FOR NICOLA

— L M

PENGUIN WORKSHOP
Penguin Young Readers Group
An Imprint of Penguin Random House LLC

Text copyright © 2009 by Liane Moriarty.
Cover illustration copyright © 2018 by Rebecca Mock.
All rights reserved. First published in 2009 as
Nicola Berry: Earthling Ambassador by Grosset & Dunlap.
This edition published in 2018 by Penguin Workshop,
an imprint of Penguin Random House LLC,
345 Hudson Street, New York, New York 10014.
PENGUIN and PENGUIN WORKSHOP are trademarks of
Penguin Books Ltd, and the W colophon is a trademark of
Penguin Random House LLC. Printed in the USA.

Cover illustration by Rebecca Mock
Design by Sara Corbett
The text in this book is set in Surveyor.

The Library of Congress has cataloged the Grosset & Dunlap
edition under the following Control Number: 2008043830

ISBN 9781524788087   10 9 8 7 6 5 4 3 2 1

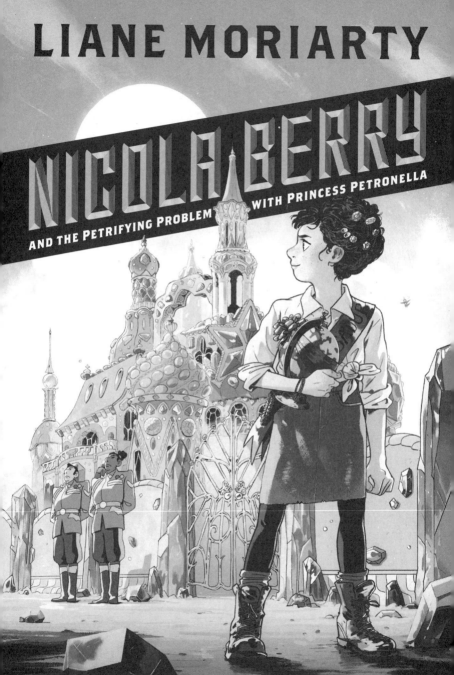

PROLOGUE

**NDER THE LIGHT OF TWO TURQUOISE MOONS** and a blazing starlit sky, a family relaxed peacefully in their backyard swimming pool.

The son was asleep, curled up on the water's surface, his thumb jammed in his mouth.

The daughter floated flat on her stomach reading a book and trailing one hand back and forth through the fizzy pink water.

The parents bobbed upright, sipping giant cups of blueberry tea while they watched the evening news on a large screen at the end of the pool. They frowned and made *tch!* noises as a redheaded princess wearing a rather grubby gown shook her head forcefully at the camera.

"She won't budge," said the mother.

"She's a spoiled brat," said the father.

"I hope you're not talking about me." Their daughter didn't lift her eyes from her detective book.

"Of course not! We're talking about the princess," said the father. "She wants to destroy a planet!"

"Which one?"

"Earth," answered the mother.

The daughter sat up straight, her book forgotten. "Earth! That cute little planet where you went on your honeymoon? But we're all going there on vacation for your anniversary! She can't do that!"

"I'm afraid she can," said the father glumly.

"We have to do something about it!" said the daughter.

"We can't," said the father.

"We can," said the mother. "And we must."

I

HONEYVILLE PRIMARY SCHOOL, HONEYVILLE, SYDNEY, AUSTRALIA, EARTH

ICOLA BERRY SAT AS STILL AS CONCRETE. EVEN when the fan at the front of the classroom rotated in her direction and everybody's hair whooshed back as if they were sticking their heads out of car windows, she didn't flicker an eyelash.

She was trying something new.

Mental telepathy.

Her subject was her teacher, Mrs. Zucchini, who was scribbling furiously on the board and shouting something about oceans and seas. Nicola didn't know why Mrs. Zucchini was so upset about oceans and seas. They should have made her feel cool and refreshed.

Mrs. Zucchini's real name was Mrs. Zukker, but everyone secretly called her Mrs. Zucchini. It suited her, as she generally had such an "eeeeuuuuw" expression on her face, you would think she'd just that minute been force-fed a plate of mashed zucchini. She was in a bad mood every day of her life because she disliked children and she had a severe allergy to chalk. She also hated hot weather and was particularly cranky on steamy, humid days like today. Once, Nicola had written her an anonymous note.

DEAR MRS. ZUKKER,

I AM WRITING TO SUGGEST OTHER CAREERS THAT MIGHT MAKE YOU FEEL HAPPIER AND LESS STRESSED. POSSIBLE INTERESTING JOBS INCLUDE:

1. JAIL WARDEN (IN AN AIR-CONDITIONED JAIL)
2. DOG TRAINER (OF BIG SNARLY DOGS WHO NEED TO BE YELLED AT)
3. ANY JOB IN A COLD SNOWY COUNTRY WITHOUT CHALK OR CHILDREN!

YOURS SINCERELY,

A MOST CONCERNED STUDENT

Nicola's dad said she should definitely send Mrs. Zucchini the note and then laughed so hard he choked on his ham and pineapple pizza and had to be thumped on the back. Nicola's mom said she thought Mrs. Zucchini might be offended and think that Nicola meant she wasn't a good teacher. Nicola said well, actually, that was exactly what she meant. Then her mom told her a long story about a horrible teacher *she'd* had at school, who turned out to have a kind heart and gave her a lemon meringue pie recipe or something. Nicola knew that Mrs. Zucchini actually had an evil black heart, but she didn't want to upset her mom, so she just patted her on the shoulder and said, "Thanks, Mom, that was really interesting and helpful."

Yesterday, Nicola's older brother, Sean, had told her that whenever he didn't want to be picked by his teacher to answer a question in class, he just used mental telepathy. He said this was absolutely one hundred percent true and that he would do a lie-detector test if she wanted. Nicola said she didn't have a lie detector handy, and Sean said that was her problem and did a somersault in midair. (They were on the trampoline in their backyard at the time.)

Nicola was pretty sure that Sean was making it up, but it was worth a try. She was hoping to learn mental telepathy before her birthday, which was December first, just three days away. It would be so impressive. After everybody sang "Happy Birthday" and she blew out the candles, she would do a demonstration of her amazing new skills. Everyone would be astonished. Last year's birthday had been a little dull, to be honest, and she wanted to make this one especially memorable. After all, if *Sean* could do mental telepathy, she could, too.

"WHAT IS THE NAME OF THIS SEA RIGHT HERE?" hollered Mrs. Zucchini as if they were all a million miles away instead of sitting right in front of her. She banged the chalk next to the squiggly map she'd drawn on the blackboard.

A few people put up their hands, but Mrs. Zucchini

ignored them. She didn't like it when someone knew the answer because that meant she couldn't yell. Her pink piggy eyes darted around the classroom, searching for a person who would get it wrong. Her chalk allergy made her skin red and flaky, and as she tapped the chalk in the palm of her hand, pieces of skin showered to the floor. It made Nicola itchy just looking at her.

"EVERY SINGLE ONE OF YOU SHOULD KNOW THE NAME OF THIS SEA!"

Nicola's eardrums throbbed.

"I SAID IT JUST FIVE MINUTES AGO. IF YOU DON'T KNOW, THEN YOU'RE NOT LISTENING!"

Nicola did not know the name of the sea. There wasn't even a name on the tip of her tongue. The only thing on the tip of her tongue was a frosty strawberry sensation from the ice pop she'd had at lunchtime.

If ever she needed mental telepathy, it was now.

She tried as hard as she could to beam her thoughts directly into the dark, swirly depths of Mrs. Zucchini's brain: *Don't pick me. Don't pick me. Don't pick me. Pick Greta Gretch. Pick Greta Gretch. Pick Greta Gretch.*

Greta Gretch was Nicola's worst enemy. (Everyone knew Nicola and Greta couldn't stand each other because they'd had some rather loud arguments in front of the whole class. Nicola found Greta to be one of the bossiest, most annoying people she'd ever met.) Unfortunately, Greta was waving her hand frantically like a drowning swimmer, so Mrs. Zucchini was pretending not to see her.

Nicola saw Mrs. Zucchini dart a suspicious look at Tyler Brown. Tyler was one of Nicola's best friends and he was smart. Nicola guessed he probably knew the answer but was deliberately not putting up his hand. He looked back at Mrs. Zucchini with wide innocent eyes behind his round glasses and scrunched up his forehead as though he was trying to remember the name of the sea. Mrs. Zucchini would be thrilled to catch Tyler out with a wrong answer, but would she take the risk? What if Tyler was bluffing?

Don't pick me. Don't pick me. Pick Tyler! Don't say Nicola Berry. Don't say Nicola Berry. Say Tyler Brown. Don't say . . .

"NICOLA BERRY!"

Nicola nearly jumped out of her skin. She couldn't believe it. She had been convinced the mental telepathy was working. It just went to show you couldn't trust a single word her brother said.

"Up to the blackboard, young lady!" Mrs. Zucchini could tell by the expression on Nicola's face she had a winner (in other words, a loser). She brandished the chalk. "Write down the name of the sea right here! If you've been listening, it should be a snap!"

Nicola sneaked a look over to the far side of the classroom and saw her other best friend, Katie Hobbs. Her face was filled with despair, as if Nicola had been sent off to fight in a dangerous battle. Katie's heart was as soft as marshmallow.

Nicola looked back to Tyler, who was slumped back in his chair as if he was all set for a midday nap. Hmmph! *He* wasn't very sympathetic! She stood up slowly behind her desk. Her arms and legs felt all droopy, like stretched-out Silly Putty.

"Oh, dear, you poor thing, I'm *so* sorry, it's such a terrible *effort* to walk *all* the way to the blackboard!" Mrs. Zucchini mocked.

Nicola looked back at Tyler and saw that he'd slumped even farther in his seat and was tipping his head back and squeezing his neck with both hands. What was he *doing*? Was he making fun of her? Nicola shot him an "I'll get you later" look, but then she saw his eyes rolling about wildly. Was he trying to tell her something? He shut his eyes and stuck his tongue out the side of his mouth as if he were playing dead.

Dead.

DEAD!

Of course! Part of her brain must have been listening after all. The answer was the *DEAD SEA*!

Apparently the Dead Sea had the saltiest water in the world. It was so salty, floating was incredibly easy. People bobbed happily about like corks and you could lie on top of the water as easily as lying on a boogie board. Nicola remembered thinking that this was one of the more interesting things Mrs. Zucchini had ever said and that she'd quite like to try swimming in the Dead Sea.

Nicola grinned to let Tyler know she got the message and went to take the chalk from Mrs. Zucchini's outstretched hand. Then she saw Mrs. Zucchini's face had turned a deep, triumphant purple.

"TYLER BROWN! DID YOU JUST GIVE NICOLA BERRY THE ANSWER? HAVE I JUST CAUGHT THE TWO OF YOU . . . CHEATING?"

Nicola saw Tyler blink rapidly, and Katie press her fingers to her mouth. Her own knees started to shake.

And that's when it happened.

There was a loud, urgent tapping on the classroom door. *RAP-A-TAP! RAP-A-TAP!*

Everybody turned to look and suddenly the air in the classroom felt different, like that magical moment just after the lights on a Christmas tree have been turned on.

Something fantastic and unexpected and unusual was about to happen. Nicola was sure of it.

HERE WAS A MAN TAPPING ON THE DOOR, BUT
he wasn't someone boring like hairy-eared Mr.
Nix, the school principal, come to give them a
long lecture about "responsibility" and "community spirit" and picking up orange peels on the
playground.

No, this man looked quite . . . interesting.

It wasn't his clothes that were interesting. He was just
wearing an ordinary suit and tie. His face wasn't especially
unusual, either. He just had an ordinary face—like someone's dad. (Although he did have one of those extra large,
bristly mustaches that can sometimes bring on a horrendous attack of the giggles if you look at it for too long.)

The thing that was so interesting about this man was
that he was incredibly, incredibly *tall*. He was so tall that he
had to bend almost in half to put his head through the door.

"Sit back down, Nicola!" hissed Mrs. Zucchini as if
Nicola shouldn't have been out of her place. Nicola practically danced back to her seat. She noticed Tyler sitting
up very straight and alert, while Katie's eyes were round
with surprise.

"Can I help you?" snapped Mrs. Zucchini.

"Oh, I doubt that very much." The man's voice was as smooth as a warm caramel sundae.

"Well, but I haven't been notified about any visitors today! Who are you? What do you want?"

"My name is Georgio Gorgioskio, and I've traveled from the other side of the galaxy on a very important, top secret mission that doesn't concern you. Now, if you don't mind, I'm going to have to kneel down. The ceilings on your planet are disgracefully low, aren't they?"

With that, Georgio knelt down and somehow managed to shuffle quite gracefully into the classroom on his knees. The top hairs of his head lightly grazed the lightbulb.

He inclined his head politely at the class.

"I'm afraid, ah, Madam, I must respectfully ask you to leave," said Georgio to Mrs. Zucchini. "My business only concerns your students. Please remove yourself."

There was a gentle ripple of pleased *huh!* and confused *huh?* sounds around the classroom.

Mrs. Zucchini's face reminded Nicola of a pot about to boil over. "I don't know who you are, or where you have come from," she spluttered. Tiny balls of spit flew from her mouth in all directions. "But I will certainly *not* be leaving this classroom! This is my classroom! You have no right to order me around, you, you—*beanpole!*"

Up until then, Georgio had been listening with a courteous, mildly interested expression, but at the word *beanpole*, his face changed.

"DON'T YOU EVER, EVER CALL ME A BEANPOLE, YOU DREADFUL ZUCCHINI-FACED WOMAN!" He extended one long arm, grabbed Mrs. Zucchini by the throat, and thrust her from the classroom like a rag doll.

The class erupted.

The bad boys in the back thumped their fists on their desks and gave each other high fives, yelling, "GO GEORGIO!" Even the really good students in the front clapped and cheered politely.

"Thank you! Why, thank you!" Georgio looked quite touched and gave a little bow. "Now, if I could ask for your attention."

Instantly the class was quiet. It was the sort of quiet that Mrs. Zucchini only experienced in her dreams.

Georgio paused for a moment and then he lifted his chin. His bright blue eyes blazed and he held his hands out wide. "I am here to find the Earthling Ambassador."

Everyone stared at him. They had no idea what he was talking about, but it certainly sounded intriguing.

Georgio looked annoyed. "DIDN'T YOU HEAR ME? I'M HERE TO FIND THE EARTHLING AMBASSADOR!" he thundered.

There was silence. Nobody knew what to say.

Georgio dropped his arms. "I see you don't keep up with current affairs. Well, I'll be brief. I'm currently testing all school-age children throughout the world to see if I can find the one qualified to take on the role of Earthling Ambassador. If I find the Ambassador, he or she will then join me on a top secret intergalactic mission."

Greta Gretch's hand shot straight in the air and she waved it about madly.

Georgio looked startled, as if he'd never seen such a thing before. "Are you all right?" he asked worriedly. "Do you suffer from some sort of medical condition? I'm afraid I'm not very good with that sort of thing."

"I just wanted to ask a question," said Greta. "What qualifications do you need for the position of Earthling Ambassador? It's just that I'm class president, so I have excellent leadership abilities."

"I was just *getting* to that, you strange girl!" said Georgio. "I am the president of a rather exclusive committee comprised of some of the most highly intelligent, astute thinkers you're ever likely to meet. Together we have come up with a very complex, very clever testing process to help pinpoint exactly the right person to undertake this mission. I won't explain more because trying to understand would make your little brains explode, which would be messy. All you need to know is that we believe there is only *one* child on this *entire planet* with the necessary qualities to successfully complete the mission. So far, I have tested over two billion, three hundred forty-two thousand children without success! That means I have—" He did some quick calculations on his fingers, muttering to himself. "—over four trillion, five hundred twenty-three children to go!"

For a moment he seemed depressed at the thought of all those children still to be tested, but then he brightened. "Who knows!" he cried. "The Earthling Ambassador might be in this very classroom sitting right in front of me! The Earthling Ambassador could, for example, be YOU!" He pointed at Lizbeth-Ann Roberts, who was extremely pretty and in love with herself.

Everybody stared jealously at Lizbeth-Ann as she flicked her ponytail and batted her eyelashes. Georgio narrowed his eyes and gave Lizbeth-Ann another look. He frowned in distaste. "Although I rather doubt it," he said, and Lizbeth-Ann pouted.

"ENOUGH DILLYDALLYING!" shouted Georgio. "Let the testing begin! Everybody to your feet! In just a few minutes we will know if the Earthling Ambassador is in THIS CLASSROOM!"

**VERYBODY STOOD QUIETLY AT HIS OR HER DESK.**
Nicola's heart pounded like she was at the very
top of a roller-coaster ride.

She looked over at Tyler, who was standing
stiffly at attention, as if he were in an army
parade. Nicola knew that Tyler would want to be the Earthling Ambassador so badly he probably had a headache.
When Georgio had said the words "intergalactic mission,"
Tyler's chin had jerked up and the tips of his ears had
gone bright red. Tyler's dream was to be an astronaut. He
was always saying things like, "I can't wait to get off this
planet," and he kept writing to NASA, asking for a part-
time after-school job.

He was also very intelligent, and although he wasn't
necessarily very brave, Nicola thought he would be a great
Earthling Ambassador. She hoped he got it. She hoped
Greta Gretch *didn't* get it.

"This is how it will work." Georgio pulled a large shiny
red notebook from his pocket. "I shall be asking ten questions. If your answer to any question is *no*, then you must
sit down immediately. If your answer is *yes*, then you may

remain standing. If, by some remarkable chance, there is still one child standing when I ask my last question, then he or she is the Earthling Ambassador!

"THERE WILL BE NO CHEATING!" he boomed so ferociously that they all jumped. "I will KNOW if you are cheating!

"First question! Do you have the letter *r* in your first or last name? Sit down if the answer is no! Middle names do *not* count! Nicknames do *not* count!"

After thinking furiously for a few seconds, about fourteen people slumped miserably back into their seats. Nicola thought happily about the two *r*s in Berry. At least she wasn't one of the first people to be eliminated.

Nicola guessed Katie was probably only pretending to be sad when she sat down. Katie didn't even like leaving Honeyville to go into the city on the train, so she probably wouldn't be much good on an intergalactic mission.

Bruno Ecclestson sat down, too, but since he was a nasty sort of a person, nobody bothered to remind him that Bruno had an *r* in it. (Afterward, when it was too late, one of the boys *did* tell him, and Bruno punched him in the nose.)

"Second question." Georgio raised two fingers. "Do you have at least three FRECKLES on your face?"

Nicola, who had always hated the seven freckles on her nose, suddenly became very fond of them. Tyler stood rigid, his freckled face stern and warriorlike. Lizbeth-Ann tried to convince Georgio that she had an extra freckle on her tummy, but Georgio just stared at her until she sulkily sat down.

"Is your birthday in one of the following months—December, March, April, or . . . June?"

Nicola thanked her lucky stars her birthday was when it was. If she'd been born even one day earlier, it would have been in November. Tyler's birthday was in September. He sat down quickly and gave Nicola a solemn smile. It was up to her now. She had to get as far as she could for poor Tyler.

There were now just seven people standing.

"Fourth question—do you own a pet fish?"

Nicola, who secretly found her goldfish a dull sort of a pet, decided she'd give Goldie an extra fish-food treat when she got home.

Four people were left standing.

"Fifth question—do you hate zucchini?"

That still left four people standing.

"Sixth question—can you perform any one of the following three tasks: one, walk a tightrope, two, dissect a rat, or three, roller-skate backward?"

Nicola didn't know how to walk a tightrope or dissect a rat, but she could *sort of* roller-skate backward, although she nearly always fell over. She wondered if it mattered how *well* you could perform the task.

"It doesn't matter how well you can perform the task!" cried Georgio as if he had read her mind. Nicola stared up at him and she thought—she wasn't quite sure because his face was up so high—that she saw the tiniest suggestion of a wink.

Now there were only three people left standing. *Maybe I'm going to be the Earthling Ambassador!* suggested a voice in her head. *Oh, no you're not,* said another sensible, prissy voice. *Don't get your hopes up. You're not special enough, Nicola Berry! Nothing exciting ever happens to you!*

"Seventh question—do you own a purple piece of clothing?"

Nicola couldn't think straight. Every piece of clothing she could think of was a color other than purple. Her red dress, her yellow sweater, her blue jeans—they all jumbled together in her mind. What color were her socks? Weren't they all white?

She was just about to give up and sit down when she noticed Katie on the other side of the classroom behaving very strangely. She was twirling her arms in circles and turning her head to one side and opening her mouth.

"Mmmm?" Nicola was halfway between sitting and standing.

Katie held her nose and jumped up and down. Aha! Katie was pretending to swim because Nicola's new bathing suit was purple! How could she have forgotten? She stood back up and gave Katie a grateful smile.

Now there were only two people left standing.

Nicola Berry. And Greta Gretch.

Sworn enemies.

It was like a boxing match. There were the Greta fans and the Nicola fans.

The atmosphere was *electric.*

"Eighth question." Georgio turned a page of his notebook with a flourish. He looked as if he were enjoying himself. "Does your favorite beach begin with the letter *B*?"

"Beauty Beach," said Greta smugly. The Greta supporters thumped their desks.

"Buddy Beach!" said Nicola.

"Nicola to win! Nicola to win!" chanted the Nicola supporters.

"Quiet, please," said Georgio. "The next question is very important."

The class became so quiet, you could have heard a pin drop. You really could have, because Sarah McCabe dropped a safety pin and everybody did hear it.

"The ninth question is—and I don't want to hear *any-*

thing except from Nicola and Greta when I ask this question—are you good at writing stories?"

Apart from a few muffled exclamations and stifled gasps there was only silence.

"Greta," said Georgio gently, "I'd like you to answer first."

Everybody waited for Greta's answer.

"Yes," she said.

Nicola snapped her head around to stare at Greta.

Greta was *hopeless* at writing stories. They were boring, there were always a lot of spelling mistakes, and you could tell she stole lines from TV shows. Greta was good at geography and geometry and gymnastics and just about everything else there was to be good at. Nicola was good at writing stories. It was her only thing. Everybody in the class knew that perfectly well. Even Mrs. Zucchini's face became a little less zucchinilike when Nicola read her stories out loud.

"Is that true, Greta?" asked Georgio.

"Yes," lied Greta steadfastly, and looked straight ahead at Georgio's stomach.

"Look at me, Greta," said Georgio.

To look Georgio in the eyes, Greta had to tilt her head so far back she was practically doing a backflip.

"ARE YOU GOOD AT WRITING STORIES?" Georgio

roared, and his friendly blue eyes turned red with fury.

"Not really, I guess."

Did that tiny, frightened squeak of a voice really belong to bossy Greta Gretch? Nicola couldn't believe it. Greta sat down and put her head on her desk and began to cry noisily and sniffily, thumping her fists and banging her feet.

"And your answer, Nicola?" asked Georgio.

Nicola's voice had gone all croaky with excitement. "My answer is yes, pretty good."

Georgio allowed the class a few seconds of cheering before he said, "Now don't get too excited, please. I've come this far before with others who still lost out on the tenth question. HOWEVER, if Nicola answers yes to the next question, then SHE IS THE EARTHLING AMBASSADOR!"

Greta Gretch burst into a fresh flood of jealous tears.

"Oh, do shut up," said Georgio irritably. "Now, the tenth question is . . ."

 **ICOLA CLOSED HER EYES AND WAITED FOR THE**
tenth question.

"Have you ever convinced somebody to change their mind when their mind was already made up?"

Nicola opened her eyes and blinked. What a funny question.

She thought about her mom when she made her mind up that it was Nicola's turn to clean the bathroom, even though outside it was the most beautiful sunny day in the history of the world. Had Nicola ever convinced her to change her mind? No.

She thought about her dad when he made up his mind to watch some boring documentary about rock music from the 1970s, even though Nicola knew he would be snoring on the couch by the time it finished. Had she ever convinced him to change the channel? No.

She thought about her brother, Sean, when he made up his mind to use the computer at the *exact* moment she was about to use it. Had she ever—even just once—convinced him to let her use it first?

Never.

Not once.

Nicola had never convinced somebody to change their mind when their mind was already made up. Her answer was no. She'd have to sit down.

"Shall I repeat the question?" asked Georgio.

So she wasn't the Earthling Ambassador. Of course she wasn't. She should never have thought she could be. It was just so disappointing to have come this close.

I am . . . bereft, she thought to herself. (She'd been looking for a chance to use the word *bereft*—meaning very, *very* sad—for ages. It was good to finally have the opportunity.)

I will NOT cry, she thought. *No matter how bereft I feel.*

Courageously, she lifted her chin. "My answer is—"

"I do beg your pardon!" Georgio hastily flipped the pages of his giant notebook while feverishly scratching his chin. "I think that question may have been an error. Yes! It was an error! How unusually clumsy of me!"

A confused murmur rippled through the classroom.

"The correct tenth question is this—are you wearing something red in your hair?"

Nicola's heart, which had been inflated with hope for a second, again dropped like a stone. Doubly bereft! Of course she wasn't wearing anything red in her hair. In fact,

she never wore anything in her hair—*hey, wait a minute!*—
EXCEPT FOR TODAY!

While she was eating her breakfast that morning, her
mother had said, "Why don't you ever wear that pretty
butterfly clip Nana gave you?" And she'd picked up the
clip from where Nicola had left it lying on the coffee table,
pinned it to Nicola's hair, and said, "There! That looks so
pretty and it keeps the hair out of your eyes!" Truth be
told, Nicola didn't really like the clip all that much and had
meant to take it out before she left for school, but she'd
forgotten.

"And your answer is?" asked Georgio.

"My answer is YES!" Nicola pulled the butterfly clip
from her hair triumphantly and held it up high.

Georgio performed an extremely strange little jig
on his knees (which must have hurt), flapping his arms
like a chicken and slapping his hands against his thighs.
"WHOOPEEEE! I've finally found the Earthling Ambassador. It's YOU, Nicola Berry! It's YOU!"

5

I **CAN'T BE THE EARTHLING AMBASSADOR, THOUGHT** Nicola. *It's a mistake. In a minute they'll realize it's a mistake and then everyone will laugh at me!*

The first time she'd been on the Demon rollercoaster ride had been terrifying and exciting all at the same time. That was how she felt now, except she wasn't screaming, of course, she was just smiling so hard her face hurt.

Both Nicola *and* Greta supporters were clapping and cheering. Greta had fainted when she heard Nicola was the Earthling Ambassador and was lying on the floor, one hand to her forehead, demanding someone bring her a glass of lemonade. The other kids were pretending not to hear, stepping over her to get to Nicola. All the girls were bunched around Nicola in a big circle, trying to hug her, while the boys were shaking her hand and giving her friendly punches on the shoulder.

"Good one, Nic!" said Bruno.

"Ow! Thanks, Bruno."

"You've always been my best friend!" said Lizbeth-Ann.

"I have not." Nicola rolled her eyes at Katie, whose face was still flushed with excitement.

"Congratulations, Nicola," said Tyler seriously. "I knew you'd beat Greta."

Even though he must have been so jealous, he was still being nice. Nicola was impressed. She didn't know if she could have been that mature if Tyler had gotten something she'd really wanted.

Georgio had stopped doing his chicken dance after he knocked over everything on Mrs. Zucchini's shelf with his elbows. Now he'd switched to a very businesslike manner. He dropped his chin and seemed to be muttering something into the top button of his shirt.

"That's right, Plum, I've found her," Nicola heard him say. "Yes, it is quite a relief. You'd better get here right away, before the press gets wind of it. Oh—and send over the Wardrobewhizonic Ladies, please!"

"I hope you haven't got any plans for the next few days, Nicola." Georgio lifted his chin from his shirt and looked down at her. "We need you to go on a little trip."

"She's got a math test tomorrow," cried out Greta from the floor.

"Good Lord! How do you stand her?" asked Georgio, and everybody shrugged.

"Where is she? Where is she?" A group of pretty,

rather plump women dressed in metallic silver overalls with gigantic *W*s across their backs marched into the classroom carrying silver suitcases. Although they were as tall as ordinary basketball players, they only came up to Georgio's waist.

"Ah, Wardrobewhizonics, at last," said Georgio. "Excellent. I need you to make her look *extraordinary*. Like a princess. Or a pop star. Or an outlaw. Or whatever she chooses, but it must be suitable for swimming. Oh, and please get rid of that dreadful school uniform."

"Well, *obviously* the school uniform has to go! We're not silly, Georgio," said one of the ladies briskly. "Hello, dear. Congratulations. Princess, pop star, or outlaw?"

Nicola thought for a second. She'd like to *look* like a pop star, but what if that meant she had to sing? Singing was her next worst thing after gymnastics.

"Um. Princess."

"Good choice. Actually, that was your only choice. We don't approve of pop stars. Or outlaws, for that matter. What's your favorite color?"

"Blue," answered Nicola.

"Such an agreeable color," the lady said approvingly, and turned to Georgio. "Could we have some privacy now, please?"

"Of course. I'll see you in a minute, Nicola. You can

choose one friend to stay with you while you have your wardrobe done, but everybody else, up to the school yard, please," said Georgio.

Nicola chose Katie to stay. Georgio nodded his approval and shuffled out of the classroom on his knees. He ducked his head under the door frame and stood up. The whole class followed him, sprinting to keep up as he strode away on his long legs.

In a moment the classroom was quiet and empty, except for Nicola, Katie, and the Wardrobewhizonics.

"Right, let's get cracking," said the lady who seemed to be in charge. "What do you think of these?"

She opened one of the suitcases and pulled out an entire rack of beautiful blue dresses, while the other ladies bustled about setting up a washbasin, hair dryers, makeup cases, and ironing boards.

Ten minutes later, one of the ladies held up a full-length mirror. "What do you think?"

Nicola's mouth dropped when she saw herself. "You do look like a princess!" said Katie. "Greta is going to *die*!" Nicola's out-of-control curly brown hair was silky-smooth-straight and she was wearing a glossy pink lip color and shimmery eye shadow. Her dress was a rich royal-blue satin, with a big full skirt that rustled and swirled around her legs. A sash of crimson fabric with the words EARTHLING

AMBASSADOR was draped diagonally across one shoulder.

"Naturally, this dress is perfect for swimming," said one of the ladies.

"I beg your pardon?" said Nicola. "I wouldn't swim in this!"

"Well, you could hardly swim *without* it!" giggled the ladies.

Nicola and Katie looked at each other, completely perplexed, but there was no time to get to the bottom of it because all of a sudden the ladies were looking at their watches, shaking their heads, and frowning as they slammed shut their silver suitcases. "Quick sticks!" they cried. "Up to the school yard! The helicopter will be waiting!"

The Wardrobewhizonics hurried off and Nicola and Katie ran to keep up with them. Nicola had to lift up the heavy skirt of her dress with both hands so it was above her knees. Her dress might be perfect for swimming, but it wasn't that great for running. As they ran through the corridors they saw all the classrooms were deserted.

"The whole school must be up there!" panted Katie. "Everyone's going to be looking at you! Are you scared?"

"Yes," said Nicola as they pounded around the corner and caught sight of the yard packed with hundreds of students and teachers. "I'm very scared! I wish you were coming with me."

"So do I," replied Katie. "Sort of."

"Oh dear," said Nicola. Their school principal, Mr. Nix, was walking purposefully toward them.

"Nicola!" Mr. Nix's hairy eyebrows leaped up and down like trampolining caterpillars. "I assume you're wondering if you have my permission to leave in the middle of a school day and attend this, this—*special mission.*"

Actually, Nicola hadn't been wondering that at all.

"Well, you *do* have my permission," continued Mr. Nix unhappily. "I have a note here from the prime minister. Apparently *all* the world leaders are extremely interested in the success of this mission. It must be something quite serious. So you have my permission for the . . . ah . . . mission."

"Permission for the mission. Ha ha! That rhymes, sir!" cried out a boy from fifth grade.

"I'm quite aware of that, Finch!" said Mr. Nix. "Well, the prime minister will also be in touch with your parents to let them know you've been chosen for this . . . ah, task. Good luck, Nicola. Let's hope you do well. Try not to worry too much about missing out on Mrs. Zukker's math test."

"I'll try." Nicola could hear Katie trying not to giggle.

There was a loud crackle and a hollow voice boomed across the school yard. "Make way! Make way! Make way for the Earthling Ambassador!"

Nicola looked up and saw Georgio speaking into a gigantic megaphone. He was standing next to a huge helicopter, which was unlike any helicopter Nicola had ever seen. Instead of being bubble-shaped, the passenger part was like a long tall cylinder, presumably designed especially for Georgio's height. The helicopter was bright yellow with red polka dots and on the back a neon sign flashed: EARTHLING AMBASSADOR ABOARD.

Katie patted Nicola on the shoulder. "You can do it," she whispered. "Have fun."

Tyler appeared at her side. "You're going to be *great!*" he said generously. "You're the best person for the job— and that's a really nice, umm, skirt!" (Tyler was smart, but strangely, he could never tell the difference between a skirt and a dress.)

The crowd of students and teachers parted to clear a path leading straight to Georgio and the helicopter. Nervously, Nicola began to walk to it. The school band struck up an out-of-tune tune.

"Good luck, Nicola!" called out her friends and the nice teachers, giving her thumbs-up signals.

"Oh, doesn't she look pretty!" she heard a girl say. "She doesn't *normally* look that pretty!"

"Missy! You come back here right now!" It was Mrs. Zucchini, trying desperately to push her way through the crowd. Her hair had fallen down around her face and her eyes were bulging.

A policeman appeared and clapped a hand firmly over Mrs. Zucchini's mouth so that she made strange gargling sounds. "Mishie! Shtop it!"

"Madam! Nothing must interfere with this mission!" said the policeman. "It's a matter of global security."

Global security? Now Nicola was feeling even more nervous.

"Hey, Nic!" It was her older brother, Sean. He was bouncing up and down on his toes, looking excited and envious. "How'd *you* manage to get picked for the mission? Did you cheat? Did you use my mental telepathy trick? Why'd they pick a *girl*, anyway? Why are you wearing that stupid dress? You don't look like a spy at all! Do you want me to go? Just tell 'em you're too scared and you want your brother to go instead."

Nicola stopped to talk to him. "I'm not a spy and I don't want you to take my place! The prime minister is going to explain to Mom and Dad where I'm going, so they shouldn't be worried."

"Yeah, right. They'll go bananas," said Sean.

"Oh, and you'll have to take my turn loading the dishwasher tonight," said Nicola. "Sorry."

Sean ignored that. "I'd better give you some advice

because you're going to mess this up so badly. Okay, so if someone tries to, like, *shoot* you, just avoid the bullet by leaning over backward like this—" He leaned back like an action hero in a blockbuster movie.

"Yeah, thanks, Sean. Tell Mom I said thank you for putting that butterfly clip in my hair!" said Nicola as she moved away, leaving Sean demonstrating moves from his kung fu for beginners class.

"Nic! Ask them if they need a kung fu expert to come with you!"

Nicola ignored him and kept on walking. She noticed Greta in the crowd, gesturing grandly as she talked to a woman who was writing something furiously in a notebook.

Suddenly a jostling crowd of reporters surrounded Nicola, waving microphones in her face. There were television cameras and bright lights that made her blink.

"Nicola! How do you feel about being the Earthling Ambassador?"

"I feel very . . . ," began Nicola.

"Do you feel confident you'll succeed in your mission?"

"Well, I don't actually know what the mission—"

"We've heard that Greta Gretch was a special friend of yours and you felt particularly bad that you beat her. Is that true?"

Nicola nearly choked. "That's not—"

"ENOUGH! This child has more important things to do than talk with you!"

Georgio reached down and smoothly scooped Nicola up into the air above the reporters and inside the helicopter.

"Hello, madam," said the pilot from the front seat. She had a long ponytail, sunglasses, and seemed to be about the same height as Georgio. "My name is Plum. It's a pleasure to meet you. Buckle up!"

Nicola buckled up her seat belt, while Georgio ran around to the other side of the helicopter, bending nearly in half so that the spinning propeller blades didn't chop off his head. He jumped in the other side and began doing up his own seat belt.

He smiled down at Nicola. "Ready, Ambassador?"

"Yep," said Nicola, pretending to be brave.

"Ready for liftoff, Plum!" said Georgio.

"Right you are, sir!"

The helicopter clattered noisily and Nicola felt a strange sensation in her stomach as it lifted off the ground and hovered in the air. She looked out the window at the people below becoming smaller and smaller as the helicopter rose higher into the sky.

There were the Wardrobewhizonics climbing into their own hot-pink helicopter.

There were Katie and Tyler jumping up and down and waving.

There was Greta Gretch sobbing into a can of lemonade.

There were Sean and his friends, leaping around, falling dramatically to the ground as they pretended to shoot one another with imaginary guns.

There was Mrs. Zucchini, kicking and shouting as four burly policemen carried her away.

There was Mr. Nix, trying to talk into Georgio's megaphone and toppling over backward because it was too big for him.

And then Nicola couldn't recognize anyone anymore. They were just busy little ants all running back and forth on the rectangular patch of grass in the school yard.

Georgio bent down and spoke quietly in her ear. "And so the mission begins."

EORGIO, MAY I ASK A QUESTION?" ASKED
Nicola as the helicopter skimmed fat cottonlike
clouds.

"If it's an intelligent one. I have a policy of
answering only intelligent questions."

"Well, I was just wondering, what *is* this mission I'm
on? What exactly will I have to do? What if I can't do it?
Are you sure I'm the best person for the job? Will anybody
try to kill me?"

Nicola's voice came out funny on the last question.
She felt breathless, as if she'd been running. Oh dear, she
hoped she wasn't going to start hyperventilating like her
cousin Ellie did when she got too nervous about something.
She'd have to breathe into a paper bag. Would Georgio even
have a paper bag? What sort of person starts a top secret
mission by breathing into a paper bag? Her brother would
say a cowardly custard one.

"I do believe you just asked five questions," said
Georgio. "Fancy a lollipop?"

"I beg your pardon?" Nicola blinked.

"I find a lollipop always helps me concentrate and, as I'm

about to answer at least some of those intelligent questions, I thought it might be nice if you enjoyed a Choc-Chip-Coconut-and-Cream Tropical Delight at the same time."

"Well, okay, thank you very much," said Nicola. Georgio rummaged around in his pocket and pulled out a gigantic lollipop, unwrapped it, and handed it to Nicola. It was as big as her face, and when she took her first lick, her tastebuds almost fainted with pleasure.

"This is . . . *delectable*," she said.

Georgio smiled. "Shall I begin?"

"Yes, please."

Georgio took a breath. "Nicola," he said solemnly, "you may have noticed that I am above average height."

Nicola managed to keep a straight face.

"Quite obviously," he continued, "I come from another planet."

Nicola had—quite obviously—never met anyone from an other planet before, and she very nearly pulled a cross-eyed look and said "Yeah, right!" just like Sean did whenever he heard something he didn't believe. But then Nicola remembered she'd left her school in a helicopter with the prime minister's permission, so she kept quiet and sucked her lollipop.

"Both Plum and I—and this helicopter, in fact—are from the very famous and very beautiful planet of Globagaskar.

We are proud Globagaskarians, just as you, no doubt, are a proud Earthling." Georgio gave Nicola a rather pitying look before going on.

"Now, the main difference between Globagaskar and your dear little planet is simply this—we're approximately two million years ahead of you. That's why we're so much taller than you and our technology is two million times more advanced, our food is two million times more delicious, and so on and so forth. We've always known of your existence, but of course, one of the most adorable things about your planet is that most of you seem to believe you're the only inhabited planet in the galaxy. We didn't want to upset you by spoiling your sweet little illusions!"

Nicola felt embarrassed for slow old Earth. "I'm sure we're about to discover you any minute!" she said. "We do have spaceships, you know."

Georgio guffawed. "Those sweet toys? Oh, Nicola, please don't make me laugh. This is far too serious!"

He composed himself. "Now, Earth has always been a popular vacation destination for many Globagaskarians. It's advertised with the slogan: 'A simpler, sweeter part of the galaxy.' Of course, we can't come too often because we do have to find remote deserts to hide our spaceships in, and we do tend to attract attention because of our height. People are always photographing us with their mobile phones, and representatives from a group called something like the Guinness Recorders keep giving us their business cards. That's why a strict limit has been placed on the number of us traveling to Earth. There's quite a waiting list, because only one family is allowed to visit Earth at a time so we don't create too much of a sensation. My wife and I were fortunate enough to come on our honeymoon. Actually, she wanted to go to one of those luxurious, modern planets, but I teach intergalactic history and culture at the local university, and the more I'd studied Earth, the more it fascinated me. So I managed to persuade her. Well! My wife had to eat her words! We had the time of our lives. We've been planning to bring our children next year for our wedding anniversary. That's why we were so cross when we first heard about the plans to turn your planet into an intergalactic garbage can."

"I beg your pardon?" Nicola let the lollipop drop from her mouth. "Did you just say a . . . *garbage can*?"

"Yes, it's really very unfortunate. You see, our king and queen have gone off on vacation and they've left their young daughter, Princess Petronella, in charge. She's about the same age as you. The princess has been making some rather odd decisions. She's determined that she's bored with recycling and she'd rather have an intergalactic garbage can. The plan is to send down a planet renovation team to make the necessary changes. I'll guess they'll have to scoop out a big hole in the middle. Of course, eventually they'll have to get rid of all the people—"

Nicola gave a sound just like the wheezy whooshing one her grandma made when she climbed stairs. Georgio glanced at her frightened face.

"Oh, I don't mean *get rid of you*, get rid of you. Like in a *permanent* way. You'll simply be packed onto spaceships and sent to live on the Planet of Bore. Certainly nobody will want to stay on Earth when it's a smelly garbage can brimming over with refuse. Terribly unhygienic, for one thing."

"But this is . . . *preposterous!*" said Nicola. (Preposterous, meaning *utterly* ridiculous, was one of her favorite words, and she had never come across such an appropriate occasion on which to use it.)

"Yes, it is preposterous," said Georgio. "Especially when you consider that the Planet of Bore lives up to its name. It's the most boring planet in the entire galaxy. No seasons, no plants, no animals, no nothing really. It will be like living in a parking lot. You'll have to take a *lot* of board games. Get it—*bored games!*"

Nicola was furious. "That Princess Petronella sounds like a *horrible* person!"

"She certainly isn't behaving very politely toward your planet. At exactly six a.m. on December first, that's this

Saturday morning, garbage will start falling from the sky. Then a week or so after that, once everybody is sick of having leftover tuna casseroles ruining their new hairdos, the princess will send down the army. She thinks people will be ready to leave by then, and will go without a fuss."

"This Saturday is my birthday," said Nicola.

Georgio looked delighted. "Why, what a wonderful coincidence! That's even more confirmation that I've picked exactly the right person for this mission."

Nicola didn't think it was a wonderful coincidence at all. What sort of birthday would it be if she woke up to see tin cans and tea bags and rotten vegetables raining down from the sky? She didn't especially like it when *rain* fell on her birthday, let alone other people's garbage.

At that moment the helicopter swerved sharply and Nicola saw they were flying along the coast. She could see curving beaches and dramatic sandstone cliffs. Tiny yachts with billowing sails skimmed across the satin-smooth water. It was all so beautiful. How could someone decide to destroy it?

She turned back to Georgio. Her fingernails dug into her palms. "Can't someone stop her?"

"We've been doing our best," said Georgio. "You see, I'm president of the Save the Little Earthlings Committee. My wife and I formed the Committee when we first heard the news about the princess's plan on television. We've been working night and day trying to create interest in the cause. We've raised money with raffles and parties and dances. We've spoken at playgroups and schools and universities. We even hired a skywriter to write 'Save the Little Earthlings' across the sky. Oh, it's been a whirlwind of activity, hasn't it, Plum?!"

"Absolutely." Keeping one hand on the helicopter controls, Plum turned around. She tapped a round badge on her collar with her fingertip. It said EARTHLINGS ROCK!

"Umm, thank you," said Nicola, ashamed that all these nice people were working so hard to try to save Earth, while Earth didn't even know Globagaskar existed.

"Well, that's our pleasure, Nicola, but I'm afraid it's quite hard work getting people interested in a cause that doesn't directly affect their day-to-day lives," said Georgio. "However, I'm proud to say that last week we presented a petition to the princess with over three thousand signatures."

"And what did the princess say?"

"She folded the petition into a paper airplane, tossed it out the palace window, and demanded someone bring her a banana milkshake."

Nicola despised this girl with her whole heart.

"So, that's when the Committee came up with the idea

of selecting an Earthling Ambassador to visit the princess. At first, the obvious choice was someone in a position of authority, like a prime minister or a king or queen. However, my wife cleverly suggested that an Earthling the same age as the princess might be more persuasive. Of course, that Earthling couldn't be just anyone. It needed to be someone with very special qualities. So, the Committee came up with a list of questions that would help us identify exactly the right person."

It was as if a giant hand was squeezing Nicola's stomach. "But I don't think I *am* the right person at all! I think you should pick someone else! And those questions were so . . . unusual." She had been about to say wacky, but she didn't want to offend Georgio.

"We've made an appointment for you with Princess Petronella at the Rainbow Palace tomorrow morning at ten."

She had an appointment at a *palace* with a *princess*. Nicola felt a moment of giddy excitement, before remembering the particular princess she was meeting.

"So that's your mission in a nutshell: to convince the princess not to destroy your planet. Think you can handle it?"

"No!" said Nicola. "I don't think I can handle it at all."

Oh, why hadn't she just sat down when Georgio asked

the first question? Someone bossy and confident like Greta Gretch would have been a much better choice!

"Good!" said Georgio. "I like that self-doubt; it will make you work even harder. I dislike nothing more than overly confident people! I expect you're feeling extremely nervous right now. Heart racing, stomach churning, hands trembling, head pounding—that sort of thing?"

"Uh, yes." Nicola smoothed the blue satin fabric of her dress across her knees. That was exactly how she was feeling.

Georgio looked at his watch and glanced out the window of the helicopter.

"Well, I don't know what my esteemed colleagues would think about this, but really, what difference will a few minutes make now that I've tracked you down?! So, how about a quick dip? I find nothing relaxes me more than a refreshing swim. What do you say?"

Nicola didn't quite know what to say. Swimming was actually the very last thing on her mind at the moment. Georgio was certainly very odd.

"Come on!" He unbuckled his seat belt. "Last one in is a rotten egg!"

To Nicola's horror, Georgio threw open the door of the helicopter and flung himself out into the cold air.

7

N NICOLA'S HOUSE NOBODY WAS ALLOWED TO SWEAR, except in times of great stress, when they were allowed to say the word *frizzle*. This was their own private Berry family swear word, which didn't upset anyone.

"FRIZZLE!" exclaimed Nicola. *"FRIZZLE, FRIZZLE!"* She tapped Plum on the shoulder. "Georgio just jumped out of the helicopter!"

She waited for a suitably horrified reaction.

"Oh, has he?" Plum turned her head slightly. "Typical! Well, why don't you have a quick dip, too? It will do you good before your mission."

"I beg your pardon?" said Nicola faintly.

"What's taking you so long?" Nicola looked down and saw Georgio gazing up at her. He was leaning on the floor of the helicopter with both arms, just like it was the edge of a swimming pool, his long legs dangling behind him in the air.

"You must come in! The temperature is perfect."

"Are you *crazy*?" Nicola felt quite petrified. She was trapped in a helicopter with two lunatics.

Georgio looked at her blankly. "Have you never been cloud-swimming before?"

"No. I have never been cloud-swimming before," Nicola spoke slowly and distinctly, like she spoke to Great-Aunt Annie, who was very deaf and a little bit crazy.

"Why didn't you say so?" cried Georgio. "Everyone needs a little push the first time."

He hauled himself back into the helicopter, unbuckled Nicola's seat belt, lifted her up under the arms, and held her outside the helicopter.

"Have fun, Nicola!" cried Georgio—and he let her go.

"AAAAAAUUUUUUUGGGGGGHHHHHHHHHHH!" Nicola's eyes were squeezed shut in sheer terror as she plummeted through the air.

Once, she'd fallen out of a tree in her backyard and had broken her arm. That had really hurt, but she guessed this was really, *really* going to hurt.

Any second now she would slam straight into the ground!

Any second now she would be shattered like a broken cup.

Any second now.

Actually, it did seem to be taking quite a long time.

And it didn't really feel like she was falling. It felt more like she was floating.

She risked opening one eye and then immediately opened the other one.

The most amazing thing had happened! The skirt of her dress had puffed out like a shiny blue parachute, and she was bobbing gently in a mysterious, swirling world of wispy white fog.

I'm in the middle of a cloud, she thought. *I'm swimming in a cloud!*

"Watch out below!"

Nicola looked up to see Georgio poised on the edge of the helicopter. Suddenly he leaped out with both knees gripped close to his chest.

"Whoopeee!"

It was exactly the way Sean jumped into a swimming pool. Nicola hated it when he did that because he landed with a splash like a tidal wave and water went up her nose. She always got right out of the pool and did one straight back at him. They called it "having a battle of cannonballs." Their mom called it "trying to drown each other."

It turned out that the same thing happened in a cloud as in a swimming pool. Georgio landed right next to her with a huge whoosh of air that caused Nicola to spin around and around in circles while her mouth filled up with fluffy white cloud.

"No cannonballs allowed." When she finally stopped

spinning, Georgio pointed a stern finger at her. "That was just for demonstration purposes."

His long black coat billowed out behind him just like Nicola's dress. He lay on his back and lazily ran his fingers through the cloud. "So what do you think of cloud-swimming, Nicola?"

Nicola spat out bits of cloud while she bobbed dizzily around in the air. She was feeling slightly angry with Georgio. "I thought I was going to fall straight to the ground when you threw me out of the helicopter!"

"Well, I knew you were dressed appropriately! After all, I'd hardly throw someone out without their cloud-swimming gear!" Georgio chuckled. Then he looked thoughtful. "Although there was that unfortunate incident with Uncle Dick."

He shook his head and winced. "Oh well! No point dwelling on past mistakes, is there? Learn from them and then move on! Come on. Don't just float there. Let's see you swim."

Nicola tentatively pushed her hands through the air as if she were swimming along the bottom of a pool. To her surprise, her body obediently moved forward. Air was much lighter than water! Cloud-swimming felt faster and smoother and more graceful. Actually, it felt like she was flying! She pushed her arms harder and kicked her legs and moved even faster. It got easier and easier, as if she'd always known how to cloud-swim and just forgotten for a while.

Georgio treaded cloud while he watched her and applauded loudly. "You're a natural!"

Nicola swooped and dived and glided through the air. The sun shone on the inflated blue satin skirt of her dress so it shimmered, and the air felt cool and fresh against her face. She couldn't believe that a little while ago she'd been sitting in Mrs. Zucchini's class learning about oceans and seas. Now here she was swimming in a cloud, while beneath her everybody was still at school!

"Try a belly flop!" cried Georgio.

"But they hurt!"

"What are you talking about? Belly flops *tickle*!"

Georgio held his arms and legs wide like a starfish and went plummeting into a cloud that looked like a scoop of ice cream. Sure enough, when he landed he clutched his stomach, threw back his head, and roared with laughter.

"You'd better not be faking!" yelled Nicola, who was used to that sort of thing from Sean.

She copied his starfish dive and went hurtling toward the same cloud. When she landed it felt as though her stomach was being gently tickled by hundreds of feathery fingers. She laughed so hard that tears ran down her face.

"Try a cartwheel!" called out Georgio, and he did ten in a row.

"I can't do cartwheels," Nicola said and stopped laughing. She was remembering that awful day at school when Greta Gretch had come around to the grassy area behind the school hall and seen Nicola and Katie doing cartwheels. Katie was quite good at them, but Nicola was hopeless. Greta had pointed and sneered and called everybody over. "Look at Nicola! She told me she was a *phenomenal* cartwheeler and look at her! She's the worst cartwheeler I've ever seen!"

Nicola had been outraged. "I did not say that!" Unfortunately nobody believed her because everybody knew that *phenomenal* was the sort of word only Nicola would say. She couldn't help it. She liked her long, fancy words.

"Come on, Nicola!" called out Georgio. "Give it a go!"

Nicola took a deep breath and carefully placed one palm and then the other down next to her feet as if the ground were there.

And to her immense surprise, her legs swung around in a smooth, perfect arc!

"I did it!"

"That was excellent." Georgio floated beside her and gave her a wink. *"Phenomenal."*

Nicola looked at him suspiciously. She'd noticed that Georgio sometimes seemed able to read her mind.

"Try a backflip," he suggested.

She did, and it was easy! She did a double backflip, a triple backflip, and a *quadruple* backflip!

Georgio looked at his watch regretfully. "Well, as much as I'd like to cloud-swim all day, we really should be on our way. Are you feeling more relaxed now?"

Nicola did a quick front flip, backflip, and cartwheel. "Much more relaxed!"

"Good. After all, every single person on Earth is depending on you not to fail this mission!"

Nicola watched Georgio swim through the air toward the hovering helicopter.

Every person on Earth was depending on her? Her mom and dad, Sean, her nana and pop, her great-aunt Annie, her friends, like Katie and Tyler, the nice lady at the corner shop down the road, her tennis coach, her piano teacher, famous people, poor people, people in other countries she'd never met—they were *all* depending on her?

Now the thought of doing one of Mrs. Zucchini's horrendous math tests seemed as easy as pie.

How on Earth was Nicola Berry going to save the Earth?

8

YOU TOOK LONG ENOUGH! NOW DON'T DRIP cloud all over my helicopter, please!" said Plum over her shoulder as Georgio and Nicola hauled themselves back in.

"Certainly not," said Georgio. He handed Nicola an enormous fluffy red towel that was as large as a tablecloth. Nicola wrapped it around herself and began to dab at the bits of cloud clinging to her dress, but to her surprise the towel ripped itself out of her hands and began to vibrate in the air, rubbing itself briskly all over her.

"It's an electric towel," explained Georgio, who was standing motionless while his own towel flew up and down and around his body. "Surely you're not still using those old manual towels, are you?"

"Ow!" cried Nicola as the towel wrapped itself tightly around her hair and kneaded her head. "We only have electric toothbrushes—not electric towels!"

"I'm sorry," said Georgio sympathetically. "How tactless of me. I do forget sometimes just how tragically backward you are!"

"*Tragically* backward?" said Nicola, feeling quite

defensive about poor old Earth. She was relieved when the towel stopped rubbing. It had reminded her of the brisk, rather rough way her mother used to dry her after her bath when she was little and would have much preferred to just sit around and drip-dry.

"No offense, Nicola!" Georgio buckled himself back into his seat on the helicopter. "You're hardly responsible for your whole planet, are you?" He raised an eyebrow and gave a little chuckle. "Although, right now, you actually *are* responsible for your whole planet! Oh, speaking of which, I've got two very important things to give you."

He searched in his pocket and pulled out a thick gold card. It looked like a fancy wedding invitation. It seemed quite small in Georgio's hand, but when he handed it to Nicola, it was as big as a hula hoop.

"Thank you." Nicola held the heavy gold card in front of her awkwardly with both hands. It said:

CONFIRMATION OF APPOINTMENT WITH

Princess Petronella

AT TEN O'CLOCK SHARP, TOMORROW MORNING
AT THE RAINBOW PALACE.

PLEASE COME ON TIME, OR NOT AT ALL.

IT IS HIGHLY RECOMMENDED THAT YOU BRING
A SMALL, CHARMING GIFT FOR THE PRINCESS.

The princess expected a present! As Nicola's nana would have said, this girl really took the cake.

"I have a selection of possible gifts at home for you," said Georgio. "So you've nothing to worry about—so to speak! And here's something to keep you focused on the task at hand."

He reached into his pocket and pulled out a very large, bright yellow plastic watch.

"It's a countdown watch," explained Georgio. "It lets you know exactly how much time you have to complete your mission before the garbage starts to fall."

Nicola looked at the watch.

It said:

ONLY **THREE** DAYS REMAINING UNTIL THE END OF THE WORLD—TIME TO GET CRACKING!

"I think you'll find it very motivational," said Georgio.

"Thanks," said Nicola faintly. She strapped the watch on her wrist and decided to try not to look at it that often.

Georgio glanced out the window and saw a huge expanse of red, rippled sand. "At last! Here's where we park our spaceships when we visit Earth. Terribly inconvenient."

As Nicola looked down, she saw what looked like an enormous, bright pink powder puff shoot vertically into the sky and then vanish.

"How annoying! That's the Wardrobewhizonic Ladies and their silly frilly spaceship!" said Georgio. "How did they beat us, Plum? I thought our helicopter was much faster than theirs!"

"They probably didn't stop for a spot of leisurely cloud-swimming," said Plum.

"Ah, good point," said Georgio hurriedly. "Well, Nicola, that far more sensible spaceship you see there is the one we'll be traveling in."

He gestured to a sleek silver spaceship sitting majestically in the middle of the desert. Nicola thought about how Tyler would *love* to be here right now seeing a real spaceship and thought about how she'd describe it to him. To her, it looked like a piece of giant cutlery, but Tyler would probably be hoping for a more technical description.

Plum expertly glided the helicopter down toward what looked like a parking bay on the spaceship's rim. Apparently, the helicopter clipped conveniently on to the side of the spaceship, like a small dinghy on a boat. They all climbed out into the hot, dusty desert air, and Georgio punched a security code onto a panel. A hatch opened silently and they entered the gleaming, massive interior of the spaceship. Nicola felt like she was inside a vast computer. She was surrounded by what looked like thousands of flashing lights, glowing buttons, switches, and levers.

There were signs everywhere saying things like WARNING!, DANGER!, and VERY, VERY HAZARDOUS!

"Gosh," she said feebly.

"Yes, it's my brand-new model *Mercury 5000*." Georgio proudly patted a nearby console. "It has a ten-volume instruction manual, which I haven't quite gotten around to reading yet, so I've had to hire Plum to fly it for me, just in the *interim*, you understand."

Plum went off to change into another uniform that looked more like a business suit. Her dark wraparound glasses were replaced by spectacles and her ponytail was neatly coiled into a knot at the back of her head. It seemed that flying a *Mercury 5000* spaceship was a much more serious affair than flying a helicopter.

Georgio led Nicola down a long corridor to a row of purple passenger pods.

"No space suits?" asked Nicola nervously as they buckled themselves in.

"Fortunately, we developed the necessary technology to replace those unflattering suits about a billion years ago," said Georgio. "Oh dear, space travel is such a terrible *bore*!" He wriggled around, stretching his long legs out in front of him. "Have you brought a good book to read, Nicola?"

"No," answered Nicola. "I didn't know I'd need to bring a book."

"Never leave your planet without a book." Georgio pointed a solemn finger at her. "That's my number-one travel tip."

"Okay," said Nicola, not bothering to mention that she'd never left her planet before. Actually, she'd never left her *country* before. The farthest she'd been was Adelaide to visit Great-Aunt Annie.

Plum's voice crackled over the loudspeaker. "This is your pilot speaking. My name is Plum."

"Yes, yes, we know who you are!" said Georgio irritably. "Just get on with it!" He began patting at his pockets feverishly. "Oh, no! I don't have my book!"

"Never leave your planet without a book," said Nicola in the same serious tone that Georgio had used.

"Why, that's what I always say!" Georgio looked quite intrigued. "What an extraordinary coincidence."

"Erm. Not really," began Nicola, but then Plum's voice came on again. "Passengers, please remain seated at all times during blastoff. Ten, nine, eight, seven . . ."

"If only we could watch a movie to pass the time," said Georgio worriedly. "We're about to suffer from acute boredom."

Nicola realized that Georgio was a little like her dad. He'd rather be eaten by a crocodile than be bored.

"Three, two, one—blastoff!"

KABOOM!

The spaceship filled with bright eye-hurting flashes of turquoise and yellow lights. It shook so much that Nicola held on tightly to her armrests. It felt like she was being spun around in a tumble dryer. She caught sight of Georgio with both his arms stretched high in the air as he let out a tremendous yawn.

There were three loud thuds:

Thud. Thud. Thud.

And then silence.

"Well, thank goodness." Georgio slapped his knees with satisfaction. "I'm quite exhausted. Did you enjoy your trip?"

"What trip?" asked Nicola. "Five seconds must have passed!"

"Actually it was 3.4928494092 seconds," said Georgio. "What a bore, eh? Let's hope you don't suffer from space lag. Come on, I'm sure you're dying to stretch your legs!"

Nicola unbuckled her seat belt and followed Georgio down a short flight of stairs out of the spaceship wondering what strange and wonderful sights she was about to see.

"Welcome to Globagaskar!" cried Georgio, and he flung open his arms.

Nicola's foot hovered over the last step of the spaceship. The word *momentous* came into her head. This was definitely a momentous moment. She thought about how Neil Armstrong had said "One small step for man, one giant leap for mankind" when he first walked on the moon.

She should say something similar. She cleared her throat and said slowly, "One small step for Nicola, one giant leap—*WHO-HOA!*" she shouted. Then *splat*, she was facedown on the asphalt ground.

"Yes, well, hurry up," said Georgio. "And I don't know what you've learned from those ridiculous science-fiction television programs they show on your planet, but here on Globagaskar, we walk upright. On our feet."

Nicola picked herself up. She felt so ashamed. How would she ever manage saving planet Earth if she couldn't even manage one teeny tiny momentous moment?

HERE WAS SOMETHING VERY, VERY FAMILIAR
about this place. Nicola peered about, trying to
adjust her eyes to the gloom.

"This looks just like—" She couldn't put her
finger on it.

Then it hit her. "This looks just like a garage!"

"Well, I expect that's because this *is* a garage," said
Georgio. "We've parked in the garage of the local community hall where we hold our Save the Little Earthlings
Committee meetings."

"Let me know if you need me to do any more flying
for you." Plum came down the stairs of the spaceship and
tossed Georgio a set of keys. She was dressed now in a black
leather jacket with her hair all loose and messy.

"Plum also flies an aero-motorbike." Georgio shook his
head admiringly. "You wouldn't catch me on one."

"I'm off to meet my boyfriend," said Plum. "Best of luck
at the palace tomorrow, Nicola. I hope you save your planet.
It's one of my favorites."

"Thank you," said Nicola. Oh, for heaven's sake, even
Plum was depending on her!

"Right," said Georgio. "This way, Nicola."

He pressed a button on the wall and it slid smoothly open.

"After you." Georgio waved Nicola past him. She stepped tentatively forward, then jumped in fright when she heard thunderous applause.

She was on a stage. A group of people just as tall as Georgio—some even taller—were standing in a semicircle below her, clapping vigorously. She looked around to see whom they were applauding and realized she was the only person on the stage. These giant people were all cheering for her! She stood awkwardly, biting her lip. Should she bow? They were much too happy to see her. They were clearly expecting something she couldn't possibly provide. She wanted to say, "No, no, it's just me, ordinary Nicola!"

Georgio came striding onto the stage behind her and went straight to a lectern with a microphone.

"That's right, ladies and gentlemen, it took some doing, but I have found the Earthling Ambassador. May I present the first ever Earthling to grace our planet . . . Nicola Berry!"

The audience clapped even louder. Nicola squirmed and plucked at her Earthling Ambassador sash.

"I know you're all dying to hear from Nicola herself, and in just a moment I'll ask her to say a few words."

What? Now she was going to have to give a speech? This was starting to seem more like a really difficult school assignment than a top secret mission.

"However, I would first like to introduce each of you to Nicola. As you know, Nicola, every member of the Save the Little Earthlings Committee had a hand in coming up with the list of questions that helped identify you. First up, may I present . . . Mr. Rory Racrory!"

A bald, bespectacled man stepped forward, blushed, and bobbed his head. "An honor to meet you, Nicola."

"Rory is Globagaskar's leading letterologist," said Georgio. "He suggested I needed to find someone with at least one letter *r* in their name."

"Yes, indeed, my studies show that people with *r*s in their names tend to be rational, reliable, and relentless," said Rory. "The more *r*s the better, I say!"

Mmmm, thought Nicola. *Could it be that Rory is partial to* rs *because he has so many of them in his own name?*

"Next we have the lovely Mrs. Molly Smith."

A plump, freckled lady with red curly hair waved cheerily up at Nicola. "Hello, Nicola! I included the question about freckles, because I've always found you just can't trust a person who doesn't have at least three freckles."

Nicola smiled politely and thought, *You're all as mad as hatters!*

A woman in a gauzy robe with hundreds of clinking silver bracelets sliding up and down her arms stepped forward.

"This is Ileria," said Georgio. "She's a highly respected astrologer who told us the Earthling Ambassador's birthday would be in March, April, December, or June."

"May the stars align in your favor, Nicola!" Ileria bowed deeply.

"And next we have law enforcement professional Sergeant Tom Atkins," said Georgio. "He very sensibly recommended we check for skills indicating courage, such as backward roller-skating."

A square-chested man in what looked like a police uniform gave Nicola a sharp salute. "Greetings, young Earthling."

Nicola straightened her back. Could he tell just by looking at her that she wasn't really a courageous person at all?

"Next is Pamela George, one of this planet's most reputable color experts."

A woman wearing a large purple hat, long purple gloves, and a flouncy purple dress said, "Hello, dear. I made sure we checked you had something purple in your wardrobe because research shows people who like purple are passionate, talented, and capable of achieving great things."

Nicola winced. She didn't even like purple! The only

reason her bathing suit was purple was because she'd been in a rush to buy a new one for the swimming carnival and that was the only one left in her size.

Georgio said, "Here we have our Committee psychic, Ella Bell, who predicted that something of great importance would happen on an Earth beach beginning with the letter *B*. That's why we thought it might be a clever idea to ask if your favorite beach began with the letter *B*!"

An extremely ordinary-looking woman in a skirt and blouse said, "Hello, Nicola. Congratulations."

She certainly didn't look like someone with special psychic abilities.

"And last but not least is pet shop manager Mr. Puck." Georgio indicated a man with a colorful parrot on his shoulder. "Mr. Puck suggested we look for someone who owned a pet fish because fish owners tend to be extremely responsible."

This was getting worse and worse. Nicola's pet fish before Goldie had *died* because she'd overfed it!

"It's an honor, Nicola," said Mr. Puck.

"It's a horror, Nicola!" squawked the parrot.

The parrot is right, thought Nicola despairingly.

"My wife and daughter are also on the Committee," said Georgio. "But my daughter had her soccer playoff tonight, so you'll be meeting them at my place for dinner."

"Don't forget your own question, Georgio!" called out the freckly woman, Molly. "That was the best one!"

"Ahem!" said Georgio, "Yes, well, moving right along."

"Don't be shy, Georgio," said the sergeant. "Your question was the one about whether the Earthling had ever convinced someone to change their mind when their mind was already made up."

Nicola looked up quickly at Georgio. That was the question he'd said was an error and now they were saying it was the most important one of all! Georgio gave her a barely perceptible shake of his head. He obviously didn't want her to mention it. What was going on?

"Let's not waste any more time with all that," said Georgio. "The Committee is dying to hear from you, Nicola. We have a ladder here, since you are somewhat . . . vertically challenged."

He indicated a small ladder leaning against the podium and looked at her expectantly. Nicola felt an overwhelming urge to turn around and run as fast as she could, but that would be embarrassing for Earth, and besides, they could easily catch her.

She lifted her skirt and carefully climbed the ladder. It wouldn't be a good look if the Earthling Ambassador fell flat on her face.

She tapped the microphone and cleared her throat.

What could she say? She looked down at the eager, kind expressions on the faces below. These people might be a little loopy, but they'd all been working so hard to help save Earth. They deserved a nice speech.

She opened her arms wide like she'd seen politicians do on TV.

"Speaking on behalf of my planet," she began, "I would like to express our, ummm, most sincere and humble gratitude for all the fine work of the Save the Little Earthlings Committee. I am . . . overwhelmed."

That sounded pretty good, thought Nicola, feeling quite proud of the "overwhelmed" part. She could see the lady who liked purple actually wiping a tear from her eye with a purple-painted fingernail.

"So, ah, erm, thank you." Not quite so good.

"I am ummm, honored to be chosen by you as the Earthling Ambassador and tomorrow morning I will do my . . . *utmost* to convince Princess Petronella not to go ahead with this, this most . . . *preposterous* and *petrifying* plan!"

The Save the Little Earthlings Committee erupted into rapturous applause. *Oh dear*, thought Nicola as she inclined her head graciously. If only she actually felt as confident as she sounded.

10

ON'T STARE!"

"But Mom, *look* at her! Why is she so short? What's *wrong* with her?"

"Shhhh!"

Nicola was walking with Georgio from the community hall to his house and she knew that people, especially children, were staring at her as they walked by, but it didn't matter because she was staring goggle-eyed up at the people herself. It had been strange enough seeing just one person of Georgio's height back on Earth. Here, everywhere she looked she could see giant-size people casually going about their business. There was a distracted-looking mother, as tall as a lamppost, hurrying down the street with a baby on her hip. Two men, as tall as small trees, had stopped to laugh heartily over something. A hunched-up old lady as tall as Nicola's wardrobe sat on a bench enjoying the sunset.

Actually, there wasn't just one sunset. There were *two*. Twin cherry-colored suns shone cherry-colored rays as they simultaneously sank on the horizon, giving everything a rosy glow. The houses were lofty dazzling buildings of gold, silver, or copper. Their front gardens were crammed with giant tropical flowers with heavy, fragrant scents.

"We live just around the corner," explained Georgio. "Obviously, there's no need to use the spaceship for such a short journey and I thought you might enjoy seeing our local neighborhood. What do you think?"

"It's very—" Nicola searched for the right word. "Impressive."

Globagaskar was so big, so colorful, and so *confident*. It made Nicola feel about as significant as a mosquito.

"Here we are." Georgio stopped in front of a silver house, slightly smaller than the ones on either side, with a profusion of pale pink roses as big as cauliflowers lining the footpath.

"Gorgioskio family!" shouted Georgio as he bounded up to the front door and swiped a card across a screen. "Your lord and master has returned!" He winked at Nicola. "My little joke. I'm not really their lord and master."

"Ha ha," said Nicola politely. It seemed that dads all across the galaxy made similar terrible jokes.

The door sprang open and Nicola followed Georgio into a circular room with brightly colored murals painted on the walls and a strangely springy floor that seemed to make her do a cheerful little bounce with each step.

"It's an Easy-Walk floor," explained Georgio. "It puts a spring in your step. Or so the advertisements say."

One whole wall of the room was taken up by a giant movie screen. Lying on the floor in front of it was a boy sucking his thumb.

"That's my son, Squid," said Georgio proudly. "Come and say hello to the Earthling Ambassador, Squid!"

The boy bounced to his feet and ran to his father. He was probably only about two or three years old, but he was exactly the same height as Nicola.

"Earthling!" Squid pointed at Nicola. "I want an Earthling!"

"Earthlings are not toys, Squid," said Georgio firmly.

"Well, hello! I've been wondering when you'd get home!"

A woman walked into the room. She was just a little shorter than Georgio, with apple-red cheeks and short, curly blond hair. She could have been any one of the moms from Nicola's school, except that she was as tall as a stilt-walker.

"Nicola, I'd like you to meet my wife, Mully," said Georgio. "Mully, this is Nicola Berry, the Earthling Ambassador. I've had a terrible time tracking her down but she's definitely the one for the job!"

"Lovely!" Mully squatted down to shake Nicola's hand. "Congratulations! You must be starved."

"Well, *I'm* starved, if anyone is interested! Hey, Dad, guess what, we won the playoff!"

A girl wearing a sports uniform walked into the room. Her thick black hair was tied back in a ponytail and she had sparkling blue eyes just like Georgio. She was about the same height as Nicola's dad, but Nicola guessed she was probably about her own age.

"This is my daughter, Shimlara," said Georgio.

"Hi!" Shimlara gave Nicola a big smile. "Wow! You sure are short!"

"*Shim*lara!" said her mother crossly. "Manners! You know perfectly well that Nicola is an Earthling!"

"I'm sorry," said Shimlara to Nicola. "Sometimes I just say the first thing that comes into my head. It's always getting me into trouble. I didn't mean you were short in a bad way. I just meant you were, ummm, short."

"It's okay," said Nicola. "Actually, I'm the shortest one in my class. I always have to sit right in the front row for school photos."

"Me too!" said Shimlara. "So I guess you don't like zucchini, hey? That was my question. I told Dad that anybody who liked zucchini could not possibly be the Earthling Ambassador. Mom's question was whether you were good at writing stories, which I didn't think was at all relevant."

Mully said, "I felt the Earthling Ambassador needed to be someone with a good imagination. You've got quite a challenging task ahead of you, Nicola!"

"Dad's question was pretty good," said Shimlara. "The one about whether you'd ever convinced somebody to change their mind if it was already made up! So you must be pretty good at making people change their minds, hey?"

"Well, actually—" began Nicola uncertainly.

"Actually, I sort of changed that question at the last minute," said Georgio. "Just slightly. So when's dinner?"

"You changed the last question?" Mully looked shocked.

"Well, my instincts were telling me that Nicola was the right person for the job, and the last thing you said before I left Globagaskar was to follow my instincts," said Georgio. "So I happened to notice something red in Nicola's hair and I thought to myself, *Now that's a good question: Are you wearing something red in your hair?* and by golly she was! Ha ha!"

Nobody laughed.

"You told Dad to follow *his* instincts?" said Shimlara to her mother. "What about when the king and queen first went away and Dad said he had a 'good feeling' about Princess Petronella?"

"Well, I hadn't actually *met* the princess," said Georgio defensively. "I thought she looked like a nice girl on television. That was obviously before we heard the news about Earth."

"And whenever we watch a movie you always get the

good guys mixed up with the bad guys. Your instincts are terrible!"

"That's enough, Shimlara!" said Mully sharply. "You're being very rude to your father, and even more so to Nicola."

Shimlara looked apologetically at Nicola. "Sorry! I didn't mean you weren't the right Earthling for the job. I bet you'll be great! I just meant Dad doesn't have very good instincts—umm, but I'm sure you're the *exception*! Oh boy, I keep making things worse."

"That's okay." Nicola felt very panicky. This was terrible. She didn't trust Georgio's instincts, either. There was probably some persuasive, brave, clever child in a school in Mongolia who would make the perfect Earthling Ambassador.

She started to pull the sash off over her head. "I don't think I'm the right Earthling, either. Is there time to go back and find somebody else to meet the princess?"

"Nicola." Mully bent right down and placed a gentle hand on Nicola's shoulder. "As soon as you walked in the door, I knew you would make a wonderful Earthling Ambassador. Georgio has picked *exactly* the right person. I have complete confidence in you."

There was something both soothing and compelling about Mully's voice. If Mully thought she could do it, then maybe she could.

Maybe.

"You really think I can do it?" asked Nicola.

"Really," said Mully.

"I think so, too," said Shimlara.

"Well, that's that then!" Georgio clapped his hands together. "Have I ever been wrong? Don't answer that, Shimlara. Now, is anybody else as hungry as me?"

"ME!" Squid came running.

Georgio scooped him up. "I hope you're going to be good in front of our guest."

"Nope," said Squid, and Nicola laughed. She pulled the same funny face at Squid that she did for her three-year-old cousin, Sam. Squid started laughing hysterically. It didn't seem to matter what part of the galaxy you were in; if you bulged your eyes, puffed out your cheeks, and wobbled your head, little kids would laugh at you.

The dinner table turned out to be a simple metallic oval, without any plates or silverware. In the middle of the table was a strange sort of gold hutch, with a large red button.

"Right, Nicola," said Georgio. "Have you ever used a Telepathy Chef before?"

"Dad!" said Shimlara. "Don't be so embarrassing. Of course she has!"

"Um, sorry," said Nicola. "But I don't think I have."

Shimlara slapped the side of her head. "Oops."

"They still cook food on Earth," explained Georgio.

"What's 'cooking'?" asked Shimlara.

"Well, if you paid attention in your Galactic History classes, you'd know!" said Georgio.

"Probably something boring," muttered Shimlara.

"Using the Telepathy Chef is very easy," Mully said to Nicola. "You just use mental telepathy to order what you'd like for dinner. For example, I love mandarins, mussels, and macadamia nuts. So I just concentrate on those foods. See?"

Nicola watched carefully as Mully closed her eyes and licked her lips. After a couple of seconds, she opened her eyes and pressed the red button on the gold hutch. A tray slid out from the hutch with a plate containing a rather strange but elegant-looking concoction of steaming mussels and juicy orange pieces topped with a scattering of macadamia nuts.

"Now you try," said Mully. "Just close your eyes and think very hard about whatever you'd most like to eat."

"I'm not very good at mental telepathy," said Nicola hesitantly. "I tried today with my teacher and it didn't work at all."

"Oh, don't worry, it never works with teachers!" said Shimlara. "Give it a try! It's easy!"

"Think of something extra nice," advised Mully. "You'll need your strength for seeing Princess Petronella tomorrow."

"Well, okay," said Nicola. She closed her eyes tight and tried to think as hard as she could about her favorite dinner, which was All Day Lasagna. It was called All Day Lasagna because Dad always said it was a good thing everyone liked it so much because it took him ALL DAY to cook it. Whenever he made it, everyone had to clap and shout things like, *Yay! Go, Super Dad!* as he served up each plate. Then he did a big bow from the waist. He made quite a fuss about it.

Nicola imagined All Day Lasagna as hard as she could: the bubbling lid of cheese, the paper-thin layers of pasta, and the tasty tomato-y sauce. The problem was that other thoughts kept coming into her mind. She thought about how she was in charge of saving the planet and wished she wasn't. She thought about how much fun cloud-swimming had been that day. She thought about the expression on Mrs. Zucchini's face when Georgio first came into the classroom.

She heard Mully cough and say politely, "Okay, Nicola, I'm sure it's got the message now. You can press the red button."

Nicola opened her eyes and nervously pressed the red button.

A tray slid out.

"Oh yuck!" cried Shimlara.

"My goodness," said Georgio. "Is that *really* what you'd like for dinner?"

Nicola looked with horror at the tray. There was an enormous plate of mashed-up bright green zucchini mixed with something that looked at first like ice cream, but which Nicola recognized as cloud. Next to it was a large tall glass of black goopy liquid. A label on the glass read: 100 PERCENT PURE WORRY. The only sign of anything remotely resembling lasagna was a single tomato sitting sadly on a saucer.

"The Earthling has to eat her dinner!" crowed Squid, banging his spoon on the table. "Eat it, Earthling! Eat it!"

"Quiet now, Squid," said Mully. "Don't worry, Nicola. The Telepathy Chef has been messing up recently. I think it's time we got a new one. Shimlara, why don't you order your own favorite dinner for Nicola and give her a taste of Globagaskarian food?"

"Okay," said Shimlara cheerfully. She opened and shut her eyes so fast it practically counted as a blink and then banged her fist on the red button.

"No need to show off, Shimlara," scolded Georgio.

Nicola gasped when she saw the plate.

It was her dad's All Day Lasagna. Actually it was an even better version because, to be honest, her dad's All Day Lasagna was always just a little burned on top. This was because her dad always treated himself to a "little rest" after he'd been cooking all day and would go off and read one of his big fat library books until he would lift his head, twitch his nostrils, and go running wildly through the house, yelling "FRIZZLE!" But this lasagna was perfectly cooked and next to it was a thick chocolate shake, which Nicola was never allowed to have with lasagna, because her mom said the thought of the two things combined made her sick, a fact Nicola didn't consider to be all that relevant.

"But this is my favorite dinner, too!" she said to Shimlara.

"What a coincidence!" said Shimlara.

"Oh, Shimlara-Anne," said Mully in a disappointed tone.

Nicola saw that Georgio and Mully were both looking at Shimlara with exactly the same expression on their faces that her own parents got when she was trying to explain why she hadn't got around to unloading the dishwasher, or why it really hadn't been her fault when she threw her basketball in the hallway and shattered Mom's favorite vase.

"You know better than that," said Georgio. "Reading people's minds without their permission is the height of rudeness!"

"Rude dude! Rude dude! Shimlara was being a rude dude!" sang Squid.

"Be quiet, Squid!" snapped Georgio. Squid dropped his voice but kept singing the song under his breath.

Shimlara hung her head. "But Mom, I just wanted to give her the dinner I knew she really wanted!"

"Darling, I understand you wanted to make Nicola happy," said Mully. "But you should have just asked her! You can't go poking around in somebody's mind all willy-nilly, you *know* that!"

"I'm afraid you'll have to go to your room," said Georgio. He was talking in the same deep, serious voice that Nicola's own dad used when he was angry, as if he were an anchorman on the evening news. It really irritated Nicola and she could tell Shimlara had the same feeling by the way she scratched hard at her arm.

"Can you read people's minds on this planet?" asked Nicola. She turned to Georgio. "Is that how you knew I was wondering if it mattered how well I could roller-skate backward and about everyone teasing me for not being able to do a cartwheel?"

There was a sudden, very uncomfortable silence at the dinner table.

"AHA!" cried Shimlara. "Dad has been reading Nicola's mind all day, but now when I do it, it's rude! Well, you know what that is? That's *hypocritical*, Dad!"

"Daddy has a red face. Like a tomato!" Squid looked very interested as he peered over at Georgio.

"Shimlara, you mustn't talk to your father in that tone of voice," began Mully.

Shimlara was outraged. "Mom! This is about *justice*!"

"Georgio, you really shouldn't have been reading her mind," said Mully. "It's not setting a very good example."

"It was for the good of the mission, Mully," snapped Georgio. Nicola could tell he was feeling sheepish. "Sometimes I have to make difficult decisions."

"Oh, that's just a whole lot of garbage!" said Mully.

"Yes, garbage," said Georgio. "May I remind you all that that's what this whole mission is about? Nicola's planet could be covered in garbage! Earthling lives are at stake!"

"Well, I was just trying to help the mission, too!" said Shimlara.

"That's different," said Georgio.

"How?" asked Shimlara.

"Yes, how?" asked Mully.

"Hungry," announced Squid, who was obviously bored by the whole discussion. "I'm a hungry Squid!"

He began to chant over and over. "Mom, where's my dinner? Mom, where's my dinner? Mom, where's my dinner?"

"BE QUIET, SQUID!" roared Shimlara, Mully, and Georgio in unison.

Realizing that nobody was taking much notice of her, Nicola picked up her knife and fork and began to eat her delicious lasagna.

Aside from the fact that she was on another planet with remarkably tall people who could read minds and cook by mental telepathy, this was just like any normal family dinner at home in Honeyville, Sydney, Australia, Earth.

 **H NO, MRS. ZUCCHINI'S MATH TEST,** THOUGHT
Nicola before she opened her eyes the next day.
That means sardines.

Every time she had a test or an exam,
Nicola's mother tried to give her sardines for
breakfast. She'd read somewhere that sardines were "brain
food" and she was convinced if she could just get Nicola to
eat them before she took the test, then she'd be guaranteed
to get better grades. Nicola hated sardines, so her mom
always tried to sneak them into her breakfast. She would
smear them on toast hidden under peanut butter, or she'd
chop them up into tiny pieces and put them in scrambled
eggs and serve them to Nicola with an innocent expression on her face. If she managed to trick Nicola into eating
just one mouthful of sardines, she'd run around the kitchen
with her arms over her head as if she'd won the Olympics.

Yuck. Sardines and math. Not a good day.

But then she heard a strange voice. "Good morning.
How did you sleep?"

Nicola opened her eyes and the first thing she saw was
the yellow countdown watch on her wrist. It said:

GOOD MORNING! ONLY TWO DAYS LEFT TO GO!
OUT OF BED, SLEEPYHEAD.

Everything that had happened yesterday flooded through Nicola's head. Oh, that's right. She didn't have a math test today. She just had a mission to save the world.

Shimlara was sitting up in her bed on the opposite side of the room, stretching and yawning. Her black hair was sticking up all over the place. She was wearing a bright orange fluffy button-up suit. Nicola decided not to tell Shimlara that, on Earth, only tiny babies wore pajamas like that.

"I slept really well," said Nicola, surprised. When she had seen her bed last night she'd been sure that she wouldn't sleep a wink. Instead of a normal mattress, it was just a long box filled with hundreds of tiny colored balls, like soft foam golf balls.

"It's weird. These little balls were really comfortable to lie on." Nicola picked one up and squished it between her fingers.

"It's just a normal bed," yawned Shimlara. She sighed. "I've got a galactic geography test today."

"I should be taking a math test," said Nicola. "I'm so nervous about meeting Princess Petronella, I almost wish I was back on Earth taking the test."

Last night, after dinner, Nicola had picked the present for the princess (a globe of the Earth—she hoped it wouldn't be too obvious of a hint) and Georgio and Mully had explained exactly what would be happening the next day. Georgio would drive her to the Rainbow Palace, but he wouldn't be able to come past the palace gates, because the appointment was only for Nicola. There would be lots of people waiting to see the princess, so when it was time for her appointment, she would need to talk fast.

"You'll need to be firm and authoritative, but at the same time polite and humble," said Georgio as if that was perfectly easy.

"Just be yourself," Mully had advised. "Speak from the heart."

Nicola still had no idea exactly what she was going to say to the princess. She'd stayed up late jotting down notes, but all she'd finished up with was a long list of words, phrases, and crossed-out ideas, like:

PREPOSTEROUS!
How would you feel?
Not fair.
Beautiful planet—oceans, mountains, beaches
What about the animals?
~~You need your head examined.~~

Recycling garbage isn't that hard.

Earthling deaths on your conscience.

~~Princesses meant to be nice = not SELFISH, HORRIBLE!~~

Eventually, she'd given up and gone to bed. Anyway, Mully had said it was better not to read from a script because otherwise she'd sound too stiff and formal. Nicola hoped she was right.

Then she and Shimlara stayed up for hours talking. Soon they were in fits of giggles. Shimlara told her all about the time she'd gotten lost while cloud-surfing and had floated off to the other side of Globagaskar where she'd finally crashed into the side of a mountain in the middle of a thunderstorm. "They had to send a rescue party to find me. It was pretty embarrassing."

Nicola told Shimlara about the time she and Sean had been jumping on the trampoline and bumped their heads together so hard, they both had to go to the hospital with blood streaming down their faces. "My dad fainted when he saw us and hit his own head," said Nicola. "So Mom had to take all three of us to the hospital." By the time they'd finally drifted off to sleep, it felt like she and Shimlara had been friends forever.

Now Shimlara was bouncing excitedly up and down on her bed so that the little balls flew in all directions. "No way would you rather be taking a test! I'd swap places in a second. I'm so jealous of you I could die. I'd love to see what it's like inside the palace. And your whole planet is depending on you! You'll be a hero!"

"But what if I can't convince the princess to change her mind?"

Shimlara's face changed and became very serious. "Well, that could be pretty bad. Once everyone on your planet finds out, they'll be really, really mad at you. Some of them might even want to kill you! You'll have to go into hiding, I expect. But that might be fun! I could come with you!"

"Shim*lara!*" Mully stood at the door with her arms folded. "How do you think that makes Nicola feel?"

"Sorry," said Shimlara guiltily. "I'm sure no one will mind if you fail and all the Earthlings have to go and live on the Planet of Bore. It won't be *that* boring."

"Oh, for heaven's sake," said Mully. "Now you're just making it worse. Nicola, don't listen to a word she says. Sometimes she's far too much like her father. Now, come with me, Nicola, I've got your parents on the phone calling long-distance from Earth!"

Nicola followed Mully down the hallway, wondering what her parents were going to say. She could imagine her mother saying, "You get off that planet right now, young lady, and come back home and get ready for school." Her father would probably make a bad joke.

"You'll have to stand on this chair like Squid does," said Mully. "Otherwise you won't be able to see the screen."

Nicola climbed onto the chair and there on a flat screen on the wall were her parents, sitting at the kitchen table back home. It was strange seeing the familiar old kitchen table. It gave Nicola a funny nostalgic feeling to see the old china bowl filled with elastic bands, bits of paper, coins, paper clips, and one wrinkly old apple.

"NICOLA! NICOLA! CAN YOU SEE US?"

Her dad bounded to his feet and waved his arms back and forth as if he was on a mountaintop.

"Hi, Dad," said Nicola. "I can see you."

"Oh, okay." He sat back down and drummed his fingers on the kitchen table. "Hi there, Nic. How are you? Bit of an adventure for you, eh?"

"Are you *warm* enough, darling?" asked her mother anxiously.

"Now don't be nervous, Nic." Her dad looked terrified. "The prime minister explained to us that you've been specially chosen for a top secret mission to save the world. We're very proud of you. Well done!"

"But don't worry if you can't do it," said her mother quickly. "Remember, it's not about winning, it's just about trying your best. It really doesn't matter if you don't succeed."

Nicola's dad scratched the side of his face and spoke through the side of his mouth. "Ah, it sort of *does* matter, darling. Apparently the whole world is depending on her."

"Well," said her mother vaguely. "But more importantly, Nicola, what are you doing about *clean underwear*? I mean, we didn't have a chance to pack a bag for you!"

"Yo, Nic." Her brother, Sean, had wandered into the kitchen. He lifted a casual hand in greeting as if he made interplanetary phone calls to her every day and took a big swig from a bottle of soft drink. Then he wiped the back of his hand across his mouth and sat down on a chair, putting his feet on the table. "How's it going? Have they figured out yet that they messed up big-time and they should have sent *me*? What's this top secret mission all about, anyway? Don't worry, your secret is safe with me."

Suddenly a man wearing a dark suit, sunglasses, and an earpiece appeared in the kitchen and put his hands flat across the screen.

"Security breach, security breach," he said. "No requests for details of the mission! We're shutting you down."

"Bye, Mom! Bye, Dad! Bye, Sean!" shouted Nicola, trying to see her family through the man's pudgy fingers.

"EAT SOME SARDINES BEFORE YOUR MISSION!"

cried her mother. "And don't forget to say 'THANK YOU FOR HAVING ME'!"

"DON'T LET ANYBODY PUSH YOU AROUND!" called her father. "Remember you're BOB BERRY'S DAUGHTER and you can DO ANYTHING!"

"SHOOT TO KILL, NIC!" yelled Sean.

The screen went fuzzy.

"Oh," said Nicola sadly. "They're gone."

Right then, she could think of nothing more wonderful than to be home in her own kitchen with her mom, dad, Sean, and that wrinkled ordinary old apple.

Mully put her arm around Nicola's shoulders.

"It sounds to me like you've got a lovely supportive family," she said. "Although I really wouldn't recommend you *kill* Princess Petronella—that's just my little tip. Now, I had a nice chat with your mom before you got on the phone and I've had the Telepathy Chef prepare a wonderful breakfast for you—sardine cereal with sardine milk and a nice tall glass of sardine juice! Nicola, what is it? Are you okay? Your face has turned bright green."

**OUR APPOINTMENT AT THE PALACE IS AT TEN**
o'clock, so we should be there in *plenty* of time."
Georgio turned the keys in the ignition of his aero-
car. "I've allowed twenty minutes to get there,
twenty minutes for traffic, twenty minutes in case
the car breaks down and we have to hail an aero-cab, twenty
minutes in case something goes wrong, twenty minutes in
case something *else* goes wrong, and another ten minutes just
to be on the safe side. Oh dear, I do hope we're not late!"

"I'm sure we're going to be very early," said Nicola. It
seemed like Georgio was even more nervous than she.

"Oh yes! No need to get yourself worked up, Nicola," said
Georgio. "I've allowed plenty of time for us to get there. You
just try to relax."

Nicola sucked on one of the cake-pops that Shimlara
had given her to take away the taste of her sardine-flavored
breakfast. It was a lollipop that looked like a miniature
chocolate mud cake and tasted like one, too. It made her
feel much better.

Nicola smoothed her hands over her skirt and wondered
if she was dressed appropriately. The Wardrobewhizonic

Ladies had been around to help her get dressed for her meeting with Princess Petronella, and there had been a lot of arguments over how she should be dressed. Mully thought she should still be dressed like a princess, in a similar dress to the day before. Georgio thought she should be dressed like a professional ambassador in a crisp dark suit with a string of pearls and a clipboard. Shimlara thought Nicola should look tough and scary, with a pierced nose and eyebrow and lots of black eyeliner, so that Princess Petronella would be intimidated into doing whatever Nicola wanted.

In the end the Wardrobewhizonics had come up with a combination of all three. Nicola was wearing combat boots and a ripped denim skirt, a long-sleeved white shirt done up in a knot at her waist, her countdown watch, a string of pearls, and tiny sparkly diamond clips all through her hair, and she was carrying a leather-bound clipboard.

"Perfect!" Shimlara had said. "You look like a tough, funky, businesslike Earthling princess."

But Nicola quickly forgot all about her outfit as she suddenly experienced the strange sensation of a car lifting straight into the air. She looked out the window and saw they were about ten feet above the ground.

There was no steering wheel in the aero-car. Instead Georgio sat behind a computer screen and tapped it every now and then with his fingertip.

"Left!" he muttered. "I tapped left—why are you going right?"

The car skimmed gently along without the bother of traffic lights or stop signs. They turned a corner and suddenly a yellow aero-car appeared from nowhere.

"KEEP YOUR EYE ON THE AIR-ROAD, BOOFHEAD!" shouted Georgio, but the yellow car slammed straight into theirs.

Nicola threw her hands over her face and waited for the terrible jolt. She'd never been in a car accident before and she suspected it would hurt, but the yellow car just bounced gently off them like a rubber ball, and the driver of the yellow car, a woman with a bright red flower behind her ear, grinned and shook her finger at Georgio as she flew past them.

"Isn't your car damaged?" asked Nicola.

"All our cars are made from Bounce-a-Guard," explained Georgio. "If we run into someone we just bounce off each other. Not a scratch, except to our pride! I do wonder why your planet is still making cars from that dreadful hard steel and glass and the like—then you get so upset and surprised when people are hurt in car accidents!"

"I don't think that bouncy stuff has been invented on Earth yet," said Nicola.

"Oh, I see," said Georgio. "Well, don't worry, I'm sure you'll catch up soon."

Nicola looked out the window of the car. Globagaskar was an amazing planet. Colorful aero-cars glided silently back and forth—no noise, no exhaust fumes, and apparently no accidents! The two cherry suns shone their cherry rays on the shimmering houses and children frolicked on the neat, orderly streets. Exotic birds soared through the sky, and in the distance Nicola caught a glimpse of colossal snowcapped mountain ranges.

Was *everything* about Globagaskar better than poor old Earth?

"Certainly not!" said Georgio. "I am sorry for reading your mind, Nicola, but you were thinking so loudly just then, I couldn't help myself. That's not the right attitude at all! Earth is a *beautiful* planet! I know I sometimes show off about how technologically advanced we are, but that doesn't mean you don't have one of the loveliest planets in the galaxy. You've got lots of things that we don't have."

"Like what?" asked Nicola.

"Like oceans," answered Georgio promptly. "We might have two moons and two suns, but we don't have a single ocean, whereas you've got five beautiful, astonishing oceans. You even get to swim in them, I believe?"

"That's true," said Nicola, thinking of her summer vacation on Buddy Beach.

"And you've got such funny animals! Like the elephant,

with its long trunk and big ears. And the kangaroo with its funny pouch. Oh, and what are they called? Flutterbys? No, that's not it. Butterflies! I love butterflies!"

"You don't have *butterflies*?" asked Nicola.

"No—not one."

"Gosh," said Nicola.

"So you go in there and you *fight* for your planet!" said Georgio. "You tell that Princess Petronella to leave your planet alone!"

"I WILL!" cried Nicola, punching a fist in the air. At that moment she felt like she could do anything. She didn't even feel nervous anymore.

"And could you do me a favor?" asked Georgio.

"Of course," said Nicola.

"Please don't tell Shimlara or Mully that I read your mind again."

"I won't," said Nicola graciously.

"Take a look. You can start seeing the palace from here." Georgio pointed to the top of the hill.

Nicola looked up.

Her heart pounded and all her nerves came rushing back like thousands of tiny ants scurrying over her skin.

"Oh . . . *wow*," she said in a hushed voice.

She'd never seen anything like it.

 **OW NICOLA UNDERSTOOD WHY IT WAS CALLED** the Rainbow Palace. It was a huge, majestic building built entirely of boulder-size gemstones like rubies, diamonds, sapphires, and emeralds. The cherry sunlight shining on the jewels created thousands of shimmering rainbows so that the castle was a kaleidoscope of glittering, glimmering color.

The spires and turrets of the palace rose high and proud in the sky. Orderly rows of angry-looking guards stood stiffly at attention with their arms folded across muscular chests.

Georgio cleared his throat. "Granted, it is somewhat imposing, but there's no need to feel apprehensive. Just think of it as going to a friend's house!"

"None of my friends live in places like this!" said Nicola, thinking of Katie's messy red brick house with kids' bikes and toys lying all over the front yard.

"Hmmm, yes, certainly none of my friends live in places like this, either," admitted Georgio. "May I suggest you take a few deep breaths to calm yourself—in through your nostrils, out through your mouth."

Nicola followed his suggestion as Georgio steered the

aero-car toward the gigantic iron gates outside the palace.

"Now, you've got your appointment card and your gift?" asked Georgio as he lowered the car to ground level.

"Yep," said Nicola. The gift-wrapped globe of the Earth was in her backpack and the huge appointment card was sitting on her lap.

"Well, Nicola," said Georgio. "I'm afraid you're on your own from here. I wish you the very best of luck. I think you're going to do a fine job of representing your planet."

He shook Nicola's hand solemnly. "I'll be waiting outside the gate for you."

"Thank you, Georgio."

She put her hand on the aero-car door handle, and for a second she felt so nervous she couldn't move. What if she was permanently paralyzed and stuck sitting in this car with her hand on the door handle for the rest of her life, while Earth was turned into a garbage can?

"You'd probably move when you got hungry," said Georgio.

"Stop reading my mind! It's bad manners!" snapped Nicola, and all at once she could move again. She pushed down the door handle and hopped out of the car with her head held high.

Grinning widely, Georgio gave her a thumbs-up sign and his car rose gently into the air and flew away. Nicola was alone on a strange planet, standing in front of an enormous glittering palace, and she was about to meet a scary princess and try to convince her to change her mind. It was phenomenally preposterous.

"Well, get on with it!" she said to herself in a voice just like Mrs. Zucchini's, and she walked up to one of the enormous guards.

"Excuse me," she said politely.

The guard didn't move. Nicola was at eye level with his enormous black-clad knees. She realized that the guard probably couldn't hear her.

"EXCUSE ME!" she hollered.

The knees slowly bent and a face appeared in front of her. It wasn't a man. It was a woman with gentle brown eyes and wavy hair. She actually looked a little like Nicola's great-aunt Annie from Adelaide.

"Well, hello, aren't you the cutest little thing!" exclaimed the guard, as if Nicola was an adorable baby in a stroller.

It wasn't quite the greeting Nicola was expecting.

"Thank you," she said cautiously. "I have an appointment with Princess Petronella." She held up her gold appointment card.

"Let's have a look at that," said the guard, barely glancing at it. "Are you from another planet, sweetie pie? Is that why you're so tiny? Why, I could pop you straight into my pocket!"

"I'm from Earth," said Nicola.

"Ooh, an Earthling!" said the guard. "I've heard about your darling little planet. My, you're serious, for such an itty-bitty thing! You're so delicious, I could eat you up!"

Nicola looked alarmed and the guard giggled. "There, there, I'm just joking, sweetie. I wouldn't eat you, but I sure would love to take you home and dress you up in teeny-weeny dresses!"

Nicola said firmly, "I don't want to be late for my appointment with the princess."

"Ooh, no time to chat!" said the guard. "Don't you worry, poppet. In you go. Good luck!"

She pushed a button and the iron gates slid open while a giant drawbridge slowly lowered itself across the moat.

"Thank you," said Nicola.

"That's my pleasure." The guard ruffled Nicola's hair and pinched her cheek. Nicola couldn't remember being treated this way since she was about four years old and her grandma came to visit. *Even then,* Nicola thought, *I was too grown-up for it . . .*

But the upside was that Nicola felt so irritated by the guard that she forgot to be nervous, and she walked briskly across the bridge and through a sapphire-encrusted archway.

Another guard, this one fat and red-faced, grabbed her card from her fingertips and said in a rushed bored voice, "You're number 4948, please take a seat and wait for your number to be called! NEEEXT!" Then he took a gigantic rubber stamp, leaned down, and pressed it hard against her forehead.

Feeling somewhat dazed, Nicola looked around and saw that she was in a huge hall with high ceilings and endless rows of chairs. Almost every chair was taken and each person had a gift on their lap, a desperate expression on their face, and a small red number stamped on their forehead. The numbers made everybody look slightly silly, which was a pity when everyone had obviously dressed up especially to see the princess.

Actually, thought Nicola, *I probably look even sillier, because the number must be huge on my small forehead.* She looked for the nearest free chair and realized she was going to have trouble climbing onto it because it was so high.

"You can use this as a step," said the woman in the chair next to hers, and she put her brightly wrapped present on the floor for Nicola to stand on. "I'm not sure the princess will like it that much, anyway."

"Thank you." Nicola climbed onto the chair and saw that the woman had a familiar red flower tucked behind her ear.

"I think our aero-cars bumped into each other on the way here," said Nicola.

"Oh, yes, that's right. I thought I recognized your face!" said the woman. "My name is Mrs. Gray. I'm pleased to meet you."

"Nicola Berry," said Nicola. "I'm pleased to meet you, too."

"Do you mind my asking if you're an Earthling?" asked Mrs. Gray.

"Yes, I am."

"I assume you're here to try to and convince the princess not to turn Earth into a giant garbage can." Mrs. Gray shook her head. "I read about it in *Intergalactic Geographic*. I signed that petition lobbying the princess to reverse her decision. My husband and I went to Earth to celebrate our wedding anniversary. It was so romantic! So quaint and old-fashioned."

"What are you seeing the princess about?" asked Nicola curiously.

"Oh," sighed Mrs. Gray. "It's a long shot, I'm afraid. I'm a math teacher, you see, at least I *was* a math teacher, but when the king and queen went on vacation, the first thing Princess Petronella did was make all math teaching illegal. She hates math, you see, which I just find extraordinary. When I was a young girl I was just *fascinated* by mathematics!"

"Mmm," said Nicola, thinking that if she'd had the chance to outlaw math she might have taken it, too.

"I'm wearing this flower to show her that math teachers can be fun and a little funky, too!" Mrs. Gray tilted her head to show Nicola the flower behind her ear.

"What present do you have for her?" asked Nicola.

"It's a book called *The Joy of Mathematics*," said Mrs. Gray. "Wouldn't you love to get a gift like that?"

Nicola was saved from having to answer when Mrs. Gray looked over Nicola's shoulder and said, "Watch out, young man!"

A fair-haired boy in a T-shirt and jeans was walking backward toward Nicola's chair without stopping. He bumped straight into Nicola's shoulder, nearly knocking her out of her seat.

"Sorry!" he said, sitting in the chair on Nicola's other side. He had the number 4949 stamped on his forehead.

"Why in the world were you walking backward?" asked Mrs. Gray in a rather snippy teacherish voice, while Nicola rubbed her shoulder.

"Because Princess Petronella made a new law last Wednesday," said the boy. "All thirteen-year-old boys whose names begin with *A* have to walk backward everywhere they go until they turn fourteen. My name is Ardy and I'm thirteen, so unless I want to get thrown in jail, that's what I have to do. At first I thought walking backward everywhere was pretty cool, but I got sick of it after a couple of days, and I keep bumping into people. So I'm here to try to change Princess Petronella's mind."

"Did you get her a present?" asked Nicola.

"Naaah," said Ardy. "As you've probably noticed, I'm pretty good-looking, so I reckon she'll just fall in love with me and do whatever I want. A lot of girls are in love with me."

"You're very vain," said Nicola.

"Yeah, I'm pretty vain," said Ardy in a self-satisfied way, while Mrs. Gray and Nicola secretly exchanged grins.

A buzzer went off and a computer-generated voice boomed through the hall, "Calling number 3956! Calling number 3956!"

An older couple with matching green spiky Mohawk hairstyles jumped to their feet and went toward a diamond archway with a sign reading PRINCESS THROUGH HERE. They dragged a pink pony with a bow tied around its middle behind them.

"They'll be trying to get the Green Mohawk law changed," said Mrs. Gray. "The princess legislated that any couple with more than three children had to get their hair cut and colored into green Mohawks. It's not very seemly for middle-aged parents. Oh dear, I'm afraid the princess might like their pony a little more than my *Joy of Mathematics* book."

Ardy snorted and said sarcastically, "That sounds like a real awesome book."

"Math is very useful, young man," said Mrs. Gray. "For example, I've been developing an algebraic equation to determine which number will be called next."

"Have you worked it out?" asked Nicola.

"Not yet," admitted Mrs. Gray. "It seems to be quite random. Oh good heavens, that was quick."

The Mohawk-haired couple was coming back through the diamond archway, their shoulders slumped and minus the pink pony.

"Calling number 4948! Calling number 4948!"

Everybody craned their heads to see who was next and suddenly both Mrs. Gray and Ardy grabbed Nicola's arms and pointed at her forehead.

"That's you!"

**ICOLA WALKED QUICKLY THROUGH THE DIAMOND**
archway. She had a feeling the princess might
be impatient and she didn't want to waste a
single second of her appointment. Her hands
were sticky with sweat, and the gift-wrapping
around the globe stuck to her hands.

This is it, she thought to herself, and was surprised to
feel a cool, calm feeling drop onto her shoulders like a soft
silk cloak. Everything was going to be okay. Yep, Nicola
Berry was going to save the world.

She walked down a very long narrow hallway lined
with pictures of the royal family. There was no time to stop
and look, but she did notice that there was one girl about
her own age who appeared in most of the pictures. She
wasn't smiling in a single one.

At the end of the hallway there was another diamond
archway, and Nicola could see a room with an imposing
golden throne. There was a long red carpet leading up to it.

Nicola walked along the carpet toward the throne
expecting to see the princess sitting in it, but as she got
closer, she realized it was empty.

Now what? Where was the princess?

She looked around and saw that in the back corner of the room there was a big four-poster bed with gorgeous purple drapes. It was just the sort of bed that Nicola had always wanted.

She could hear a familiar tinny sound—what was it? For some reason it reminded her of her brother, Sean.

As she neared the bed, she worked it out. It was the sound of someone listening to very loud music through headphones. Sean had received a phone for his last birthday and he spent hours sprawled on his bed listening to it.

Sure enough, there was a girl wearing a satin ball gown and headphones lying facedown on the bed.

It wasn't a very *regal* way for a princess to behave.

"Ahem," Nicola coughed politely.

The girl didn't move.

"AHEM!" Nicola coughed again. "AHEM! AHEM! AHEM!"

She was almost choking from trying to cough so loud.

Nothing.

"Princess Petronella? Excuse me, PRINCESS PETRO-NELLA?"

Was this how the princess dealt with all her requests and complaints? She just lay on her bed, listening to music and ignoring them?

Nicola wasn't going to put up with that. She did exactly

what she did to Sean whenever her mom told her to go and tell him that dinner was ready.

She grabbed the back of the princess's leg and squeezed, though admittedly not quite as hard as she squeezed Sean's leg.

"HUH?!"

The princess flipped over and sat up, pushing her headphones down to her shoulders.

"How DARE you!"

Of course she was very tall, but apart from that she looked like an ordinary girl. She had red curly hair done up in a bun, a silver tiara, about the same number of freckles as Nicola, and a sulky, turned-down mouth.

"I've got an appointment to see you," explained Nicola.

"Do you KNOW who I AM?"

"Well, yes," said Nicola. "You're Princess Petronella. My name is Nicola Berry. I'm the Earthling Ambassador. I'm here to discuss your decision to turn Earth into a giant intergalactic garbage can."

"BORING!" The princess yawned without bothering to cover her mouth. She grabbed the gift from Nicola and tore off the paper.

"What's this? The last people got me a pink pony!"

"That's Earth," said Nicola. "That's the planet you want to destroy."

"BORING!"

She was the rudest person Nicola had ever met in her entire life.

"Well, it's not boring for us," said Nicola. "How would you like it if somebody decided to turn *your* planet into a garbage can and you walked out of your front door to see garbage flying down like rain? Imagine having to move to Planet Bore because last time you tried looking up at the sky, somebody's old tea bag landed *SPLAT* on your face because that person had bad aim and missed the opening!"

"Ha!" The princess giggled. "That's funny. Go on. You're becoming more interesting now."

"Have you ever been on a vacation to Earth?" asked Nicola.

"I go to much more interesting planets for my vacations," sneered the princess.

"Well, Earth is a *phenomenal* planet!" said Nicola. She'd never really felt proud of her planet until now. She spun the globe for the princess as if she was trying to amuse Katie's little brother, who was two. "It's got everything—big countries, tiny countries, mountain ranges, deserts, oceans, and seas." She wished she'd listened more in geography—there were probably lots of amazing things about Earth she was forgetting. She hoped the princess didn't ask her to explain latitude and longitude.

"What's an ocean?" asked the princess, stretching her legs out on the bed in front of her. "You're getting boring again."

"It's like a gigantic beautiful swimming pool that stretches as far as you can see," Nicola told her. "Oceans are salty and blue and the water goes up and down, so sometimes when you're swimming, you feel like you're on a roller coaster!"

"Huh." The princess raised a nearly impressed eyebrow. "That sounds pretty good."

Nicola's heart started to lift. She was going to convince her! She was going to do it! She was going to be a hero!

"So, could you please change your mind about making our planet into a garbage can?" she asked in her humblest, most polite voice. "It's just that if you did it, we'd all have to leave and there's no space on any of the other planets to take us and eventually we'd all die and that would be a terrible thing to have on your conscience."

"Mmmmm." The princess spun the globe around and then stopped it and tapped her fingers. Nicola noticed she was tapping them against the Indian Ocean.

"Well, *all right*," said the princess. "I won't turn Earth into a garbage can."

Nicola's knees wobbled with relief. She imagined how famous she would be when she got back to Earth. She'd probably have to do television interviews. There might be a public holiday every year on her birthday, just like the queen's. Maybe her face would appear on a postage stamp. She'd have to make sure she didn't let it go to her head. "I'm not a hero," she'd say quietly. "I just did what anybody would do."

"HA HA! GOTCHA!"

The princess was up on her knees on the four-poster bed pointing her finger at Nicola and laughing hysterically.

"I beg your pardon?" Nicola felt sick.

"I PLAYED THE BEST TRICK ON YOU!" The princess's pale face was pink with delight.

"You mean, you haven't changed your mind?" asked Nicola.

"Of course not! Why should I care about a stupid planet filled with stupid short people like you? I think it will make a perfect garbage can. And I don't care what happens to all of you because I don't HAVE a conscience!"

Nicola felt red-hot rage puffing out her body. If she got any angrier, she might pop.

With her fists clenched tight, she said, "This is *PRE-POSTEROUS*! You can't do this!"

"Oh yes I can, Miss Big Words." The princess pointed at her tiara. "I'm Princess Petronella, remember? I'm in charge of this planet, and if you don't like it, tough luck! Okay, time's up, you're dismissed."

What would happen, Nicola wondered, *if I slapped this awful girl right across the face?*

"I wouldn't even think about it, if I were you." The princess narrowed her eyes.

"It's not good manners to read other people's minds," said Nicola helplessly.

"I'm a princess! I don't NEED good manners! And if you don't leave now, I'm calling the guards, and they'll lock you up forever if I order them to and I won't even have to say PLEASE!"

There was nothing Nicola could do. She'd failed. There wouldn't be any cheering crowds when she got back to Earth. Everybody would hate her. Greta Gretch would say, "I knew you wouldn't be able to do it, Nicola Berry." And what would Georgio say? He'd be so disappointed.

Nicola refused to cry in front of the princess. With her head high, she turned to go back out the archway.

"Hey!" the princess shouted.

Nicola turned around and the princess tossed her the globe.

"You can keep it," she said. "It will be a good souvenir of what your planet looked like before it became my intergalactic garbage can!"

**HEN NICOLA WALKED OUT OF THE PALACE**
gates, the first thing she saw was Georgio's hopeful face peering at her through the aero-car window. He took one look at the globe, which she carried under her arm, and his smile faded.

"No luck, eh?" he said as she climbed up into the aero-car beside him. "That princess is a tough nut to crack. No problem! We'll think of something else. I'll speak to the other members of the Save the Little Earthlings Committee after work. We'll come up with another idea!"

"What about people on Earth?" asked Nicola. "Should we tell them what happened?" She cringed at the thought of everyone she knew knowing she had failed.

"Yes, I suppose it's only courteous I let your world leaders know things aren't going so well," said Georgio, absentmindedly tapping the dashboard as they glided back down the hill away from the Rainbow Palace. "Perhaps they'll come up with another idea, but they're a funny lot. Some of them want to declare war on Globagaskar, which is pretty silly, as they don't even know where we are. Some of them want to build a gigantic umbrella over Earth to protect it from the garbage, but they've no idea how to build such a thing. A few of them still think it's all an elaborate hoax and doubt the princess even exists. They can't agree on what to do. Last I heard, the argument had got so heated, they were threatening to declare an all-out world war!"

"Oh," said Nicola. So much for hoping the grown-ups could work things out.

"Don't worry," Georgio said, sounding worried to death. "We'll work something out. Watch out, BOOFHEAD!" Their aero-car zoomed straight into the side of an aero-truck and bounced off, causing a big burly truck driver to shake his head disapprovingly.

They arrived back home just as Shimlara was getting off her school aero-bus. Georgio dropped Nicola off and headed back to the university. He said he was going to ask all his intergalactic history and culture students to write essays on how to save Earth. "Who knows?" he said. "They might come up with something, and at least it will keep them busy."

"Mmmm," said Shimlara sympathetically when she saw Nicola. "I think by the look on your face, you probably did as well as on your mission as I did on my galactic geography test."

"Oh, Shimlara!" said Mully, coming out of the front door. "You didn't *fail*, did you?" She paused and gave Nicola an apologetic glance. "Of course, I don't mean you failed, Nicola."

"Really sensitive, Mom!" said Shimlara.

"I did fail," said Nicola sadly. "I failed completely." And then she made the mistake of looking at her countdown watch. It said:

ONLY TWO DAYS LEFT—REMEMBER,
FAILURE IS NOT AN OPTION.

Nicola was starting to really dislike her countdown watch.

"Let's have a swim," Shimlara suggested. "That always makes me feel better."

Nicola was much too short to fit into any of Shimlara's current bathing suits, so she had to borrow one from when Shimlara was about four years old.

"I hope you don't feel embarrassed wearing this," Mully said, holding up the suit, which had dozens of smiling teddy bears all over it. Nicola couldn't care less what she wore, she felt so sad and dispirited.

But she started to feel a little better once she and Shimlara were swimming together in pink, fizzy water that smelled much nicer than the chlorinated water in swimming pools on Earth.

Shimlara showed Nicola how to pull a little cord on her

teddy-bear bathing suit, so it filled with air and she could float on top of the water as easily as if she were lying on top of a bed. *It must be just like swimming in the Dead Sea*, thought Nicola as she stretched out comfortably.

But what about all those people floating happily on top of the Dead Sea when the garbage started to fall? The garbage would never sink! "That Nicola Berry even ruined the Dead Sea," people would say to one another.

"So, did the princess just ignore everything you had to say?" Shimlara lay flat on her back, her hands behind her head.

"She liked it when I talked about tea bags landing on our faces," said Nicola. "She thought that was pretty funny. Actually, I think maybe she's just bored with life."

"Bored?" snorted Shimlara. "If I was a rich princess in charge of a whole planet, I would so not be bored!"

"She seemed almost interested when I told her about oceans, but then she got bored again. She's a horrible person."

"What are oceans?" asked Shimlara.

Nicola explained, and Shimlara rolled over onto her stomach and looked enthralled. "I'd *love* to swim in an ocean! When we go on vacation to Earth for Mom and Dad's wedding anniversary, I'll make sure they take me to an ocean. Oh—that's right . . ." Her voice trailed off.

"Yep, no more vacations to Earth," said Nicola. "Unless you want to spend your vacation in a disgusting garbage can!"

But something Shimlara had said got her thinking.

With a splash, she sat upright on the water.

"Shimlara," she said, "I've got an idea, and I think I'll need your help."

"Great!"

"But it's illegal, probably dangerous, and we definitely can't tell your dad."

RE YOU SURE YOU CAN'T SHARE YOUR IDEA
with us?" asked Georgio. "Or at least give us the
teeniest hint?"

It was later that day and Nicola, Shimlara,
Mully, and Georgio were all sitting around the
kitchen table, drinking blueberry tea from gigantic china
cups. (Nicola had to use both hands just to lift hers.) Squid
was kicking a ball around the house and falling over each
time his foot didn't connect.

"I can't tell you anything," said Nicola firmly.

She knew that if she told Georgio her idea, he would
immediately forbid her to try anything so dangerous.

Georgio looked at her suspiciously and twirled the ends
of his mustache.

Shimlara had taught Nicola that if you knew somebody
was likely to try and read your mind, you could block them
by reciting multiplication tables in your head.

Five sixes are thirty, thought Nicola carefully. *Six sixes
are . . . um, six sixes are . . . erm, thirty-six?*

"Aha! You're blocking me!" Georgio pointed a finger at
her. "I see Shimlara has been teaching you a thing or two.

And yes, by the way, six sixes are thirty-six—goodness me, have they stopped teaching math on Earth, too?"

"You really must stop trying to read her mind, Georgio," said Mully.

"Oh well, it's no time to be worrying about etiquette," said Georgio gloomily. "The fate of a planet is at stake and I have no idea whether Nicola's idea is sensible or silly!"

"I'm going to be there to make sure Nicola doesn't do anything silly," said Shimlara.

"Oh PHEW!" Georgio wiped his hand dramatically across his forehead. "My very sensible daughter will be involved. GOSH. That's such a RELIEF!"

"I *hate* it when you're sarcastic like that, Dad," said Shimlara. "Just because I got lost that time when I went cloud-surfing . . ."

"Did the Save the Little Earthlings Committee come up with any good ideas?" asked Nicola, to change the subject. She didn't like it when her dad was sarcastic, either.

"Well, we think it might be worth trying to reach the king and queen on their vacation again," answered Georgio. "They would put a stop to this nonsense immediately! Unfortunately, they're doing a three-month underground trek on the Planet of Doom and it's *impossible* to contact anyone on Doom, especially when they're underground. We're also trying to lobby other planets in preparation for the worst-case scenario. If Earth actually is destroyed, we'll need to find somewhere for you all to live. So far they've all said . . ." Georgio lifted his hands in a hopeless gesture.

"Yes?" prompted Nicola.

"No," answered Georgio sadly. "They've all said absolutely not. Not enough space, Earthlings are too short and annoying, Earthlings would take all the jobs, that sort of thing."

"Well, those sound like great plans, Dad," said Shimlara.

"Oooh, I *hate* it when you're sarcastic like that, Shimlara," Georgio put on a silly voice.

"Oh stop it, both of you!" said Mully. "You're as bad as each other. Well, Georgio, to be honest, I think we just have to do what Nicola wishes. After all, we're not Earthlings and she is here representing her planet."

Georgio sighed gustily. "Fine. I guess you're right. You are the Earthling Ambassador, Nicola, and we must respect that. Don't bother trying to block me, I'm not going to read your mind again. It's too painful listening to you trying to do your tables! Tell me, can I help you in any way with putting this idea of yours into practice? I'm at your service."

Nicola's heart raced. Nobody was going to stop her. She was going to be allowed to put this most *audacious* plan into practice.

She assumed her most confident voice. "Yes, please. I actually do need your help with one thing, Georgio," she said. "I need you to go back to Earth and pick up a few people for me."

17

I NEED TO GET A TEAM OF PEOPLE TOGETHER," explained Nicola.

"A squadron!" interjected Shimlara. "A squadron ready for *battle!*"

"Oh goodness," said Mully faintly. "I need chocolate to hear this." She gave the Telepathy Chef a desperate look and pressed the button, and an oversize bar of chocolate popped straight out. Mully took an enormous bite and gestured for Nicola to begin.

"We'll be called the Earthling Squadron—except that's no good, because Shimlara's not an Earthling. Okay, we'll be the Space Squad. No, no, we'll be the *Space Brigade!* That sounds better."

Space Brigade. Just saying the words made Nicola feel resourceful and capable.

Georgio blinked rapidly. "Okay, okay, I see your strategy. Many hands make light work, as they say. Of course, they also say too many cooks spoil the broth, but you're not making broth, are you? That is, I assume you're not . . . So how many Earthlings do you need me to pick up for this Space Brigade of yours? One hundred? Two hundred? A few squillion?"

"Oh, no, just three." Nicola handed him a slip of paper with the three names written on it:

Tyler Brown

Katie Hobbs

Sean Berry

"Rightio," said Georgio. He lowered his chin and started talking into his top button, just like he had back on Earth when he first chose Nicola as Earthling Ambassador.

"His top button is a Voice-Operated Miniature Phone," whispered Shimlara, who knew by now that Nicola didn't always understand the technology on Globagaskar. Although sometimes Shimlara went a bit far with her explanations. That morning at breakfast she'd explained to Nicola that glasses were used to hold water. "Actually, we do have *glasses* on Earth," Nicola had said.

"Hello, Plum!" cried Georgio. "Can you hear me? It sounds very noisy there. It's me, Georgio! I need you to fly me to Earth for a quick Earthling pickup. Can you get here fairly soon? Like, right now? Oh, it's your birthday today? You're in the middle of your birthday party? Well, many happy returns! So, how quickly can you get here?"

"Georgio!" hissed Mully.

Georgio gave Mully a baffled look and said into his button, "Wonderful! The spaceship is still parked at the community hall. I'll meet you there."

He rubbed his hands together purposefully and said, "Plum is on her way. She didn't sound very gracious about it, I must say, but spaceship pilots can be a grumpy lot! I'll be back in a jiffy."

He strode off, wrapping a giant scarf around his neck.

Nicola imagined how Sean, Tyler, and Katie would react when Georgio turned up in their classrooms. Sean and Tyler would be crazy with excitement. Katie would be nervous—but Nicola knew she needed her for the Space Brigade. She had a feeling that Katie's marshmallow-soft heart might be useful.

Five minutes later, Georgio leaped through the door and Nicola waited to hear what he'd forgotten—the keys to the spaceship, perhaps?

"I'm back!" he said. "Got them all, no problem!"

Nicola's jaw dropped.

"Plum must have convinced Georgio to let her fly at Time-Squeeze speed," said Mully. "Georgio probably spent a few hours collecting everyone on Earth, but Time-Squeeze compressed that time into just a minute. It uses a lot of rocket fuel so we can't do it too often, but poor Plum probably wanted to get back to her party."

"Nicola, I present your Space Brigade!" said Georgio. He flung an arm sideways.

Sean strolled into the room, wearing jeans and a

T-shirt, a backpack slung casually over one shoulder. "Awesome!" he said, looking around him. "So you need my help, eh, Nic? Knew you would."

Tyler followed him, carrying a suitcase and adjusting his spectacles. "Hi, Nicola. I just want you to know this is the best thing that's ever happened to me in my entire life."

Katie was behind Tyler, lugging two overnight bags, one of which was Nicola's. She must have gone over to Nicola's place to get it. It was typical of Katie to remember that Nicola hadn't been given the chance to pack her own bag.

Katie's eyes were like saucers as she dropped the bags with a thud. "Is this really another planet?"

And then a very unexpected person elbowed Katie out of the way and marched into the room.

Nicola spoke through gritted teeth. "What are *you* doing here?"

T WAS GRETA GRETCH.

Nicola couldn't believe it. Her Very Worst Enemy was here. It was preposterous. It made her want to shudder. "I never asked you to bring *her*!" she said to Georgio. She knew she sounded rude, but she couldn't help it.

Georgio frowned at Greta. "But I don't think I *did* bring her!"

"Greetings, aliens! My name is Greta Gretch." Greta lifted her nose proudly. She was wearing her Honeyville school uniform and carrying her school backpack. "I stowed away on the spaceship. I knew that I should have been the one picked for the mission, so I had to take the initiative. Obviously, you've failed, Nicola. That's why you had to send for your friends and your brother to help. So why don't you just admit that you don't have what it takes, step aside, and let me get on with the job?"

"What a horrendous little worm," sighed Georgio.

"There's a girl at my school just like her," Shimlara said sympathetically to Nicola.

"Ah, sir." Tyler practically saluted Georgio. "Do you think you could just take her straight back to Earth?"

"Well, ordinarily I could," said Georgio, "but Plum made me sign a contract promising not to disturb her again on her birthday. So we'll have to wait until tomorrow. I wonder where we can put her in the meantime?"

Sean was getting bored with all this talk.

"So, Nic, who do you want me to kill?" he asked. "Just point me in the right direction. I knew they should never have sent a girl to do the job of a warrior!"

"Now that's ENOUGH!" Everybody turned in surprise to look up at a red-faced Mully, her hands on her hips. "I'm not at all happy with this disrespect being shown to Nicola. She was chosen for this VERY DIFFICULT mission because she's the best person on your planet to do it. She has done an excellent job so far and now she's decided that she needs some help. *She* is the LEADER of this Space Brigade and you need to follow her instructions. If you can't do that, then you don't belong here and you can sit in my three-year-old son's time-out corner until it's all over!"

"Way to go, Mom!" said Shimlara.

"Yes, I was just about to say something along very similar lines myself," said Georgio.

"Tell me what you'd like me to do, Nicola." Tyler stood

up straight and looked at Nicola so respectfully that she had to swallow a giggle. "I'm ready for action."

"I'm ready for, ah, action, too, Nicola." Katie looked terrified.

Everyone looked at Sean.

"Ummm." He shuffled his feet. Nicola knew this would be agony for him. "Yeah, okay, ummm, Nic's the boss. Whatever you think, Nic."

"Now, Nicola," said Mully. "What would you like to do about Greta? Do you want her on the Space Brigade or not? If not, she can just wait here with Georgio and me until Plum is ready to take her back to Earth."

Greta raised her chin and didn't say anything, but Nicola noticed she was biting her bottom lip hard and her knees were shaking. She obviously wanted to be on the Brigade very badly. It made Nicola feel slightly sick to have that much power to make somebody happy or sad. Should she give her a chance? After all, Greta did have some pretty good ideas sometimes, even though she was generally pretty despicable.

Give the despicable worm a chance. She might surprise you.

It was Georgio's voice, but he hadn't spoken out loud. In fact, he was looking up at the ceiling and whistling a tune, as if all this had nothing to do with him.

Sorry! Just temporarily talking inside your head for reasons of privacy! Won't happen again! So, what are you going to do?

Extraordinary! Not only could Globagaskarians read your mind, they could talk inside your head as well! Although, presumably, that was bad manners, too.

Yes, yes, very rude of me! Are you going to get on with it?

Nicola shook her head distractedly and took a deep breath.

"Greta," she said. "I'm happy to have you on the team, but I've got some conditions."

"Okay," Greta looked wary.

"You have to do what I say—even if you disagree with it."

"Can I *tell* you if I disagree with it?" asked Greta.

"You can tell me, but if I say you've still got to do it, then you've got to do it," said Nicola, wondering if she was making a terrible mistake.

"Okay."

"The second condition is that if I decide you're off the team, then you're off it, NO ARGUMENTS. You'll have to go straight back to Earth."

"Hmmmph." Greta's mouth twisted. She tapped her foot and lifted her eyes to the ceiling.

Finally she spoke. "I accept your conditions, Nicola," she said grandly, as if she were doing Nicola a great favor.

"Fine," sighed Nicola. "You're in the Brigade."

"Thank you." Greta smiled, and for a moment she almost looked like a nice person. Well, maybe it wouldn't be so bad after all.

Better start acting like the boss. What's your first move going to be?

"Would you please stop talking in my head!" said Nicola, exasperated.

"Huh? What? Are you talking to me, Nicola?" Georgio gave her a confused, innocent look.

"I would like to call an immediate meeting of all members of the Space Brigade." Nicola tried to sound firm and fair, but not too bossy. She wanted to be a calm, decisive leader.

"Right," said Tyler. "Let's go."

"Where will the meeting be?" asked Katie.

"Ummm." Nicola looked around helplessly. It wasn't like she was in her own house.

"It will be in my bedroom," said Shimlara. "If that's okay with you, Nicola?"

"Yes," said Nicola sternly. "That will be fine."

"Follow me," said Shimlara. "And Mom and Dad, make sure you don't interrupt us!"

Mully and Georgio both held up their hands as if it were the last thing on their minds.

As they all trooped down the hallway and into Shimlara's bedroom, Squid worked out that something was going on that didn't involve him.

"I COMING, TOO!" He threw his arms around Shimlara's legs as she tried to close the door on him.

"Moooooom!" yelled Shimlara.

Katie took control of the situation. "That's right, Squid, you *can't* stay out there and have fun with your toys," she said, taking him by the arm. "You *must* come into Shimlara's room and sit very quietly while we talk about boring things for a long time. Come in here right now!"

"NO!" Squid's face crumpled. "I PLAYING WITH TOYS!"

"Well, okay then." Katie let him go. "You win. Off you go."

Squid ran for his life.

"You're a genius," said Shimlara, locking her bedroom door behind them. "Have you got a little brother, too?"

"I've got three of them," said Katie. "Reverse psychology works every time."

"Right," said Nicola as everybody settled down, sitting on the floor or on Shimlara's funny ball bed. "I'd like to call this meeting to order."

"Don't take yourself too seriously there, Nic," said Sean. "You might be the boss, but you're not the Queen of England."

"Are you going to start by calling the roll?" asked Greta. "That's what I'd do. Have you even got a list of our names? I mean, you've got to be organized, Nicola, no offense or anything, but I've seen your locker at school, and you're not a very organized person."

"QUIET," said Nicola. Keeping these people in line was going to be an even tougher job than meeting the princess. "The reason I decided I needed more than one person to complete this mission is because I have an idea. It could be dangerous and it's definitely against the law."

"Now you're talking." Sean grinned.

"But I think it's the only way we're going to save Earth from becoming an intergalactic garbage can."

Everybody looked at her expectantly.

"My idea . . . ," began Nicola hesitantly.

Tyler gave her a little nod of encouragement.

"My idea is to kidnap the princess."

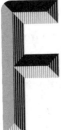OR A MOMENT THERE WAS SILENCE, THEN
everybody burst out talking at once.

"AWESOME!" said Sean.

"Oh, but that seems so *mean*," said Katie.

"But how would we ever get past the guards?" asked Shimlara.

"Is that really your best idea?" asked Greta.

"How would kidnapping the princess help accomplish the mission?" asked Tyler. "She could just pretend to agree to do what we want and then change her mind again when we let her go free. I mean, we can't kidnap her forever."

Everybody stopped talking when they heard Tyler's question and looked to Nicola for an answer.

"I think Princess Petronella is bored," explained Nicola. "She's coming up with these stupid laws just for something to do. If we take her to Earth, we can show her how fun it is! She can swim in the oceans and we could take her to the zoo and show her giraffes and kangaroos and koala bears and, and . . . stuff! And then maybe she'll realize what a terrible thing it would be to destroy such an amazing place."

"Mmmm," said Tyler doubtfully. "I guess that might work."

"The princess is probably upset that her parents didn't take her with them on their vacation," said Katie thoughtfully. "Georgio told us she didn't have any brothers or sisters, so she must be pretty lonely."

"You might be right," said Nicola. "She probably just needs some friends to help make her nicer."

"What if the princess is just a nasty person?" asked Shimlara. "Some people are nasty all the way through."

"In that case we could *torture* her!" said Sean enthusiastically.

Everybody stared at him until he mumbled, "Just a little bit—not so it really hurts her. Can't anybody take a joke around here?"

"I don't want to question your idea or anything, Nicola," said Greta. "But *how* are we going to kidnap the princess? Have you got a plan? I mean, I don't think kidnapping is that *easy*, you know. We could all end up in jail. I don't want a criminal record! It might affect my chances of being class president next year."

"Yes, I am aware that kidnapping a princess isn't going to be easy," said Nicola. "That's why I formed the Brigade. I knew I couldn't do it on my own, but I thought together we could come up with some ideas." She put on a honey-sweet voice. "If you think it's too hard, Greta, then you don't need to be in the Space Brigade. You can just go and wait outside with Mully and Georgio and Squid."

"Of course, *I* can think of some ideas." Greta looked miffed. "Everybody always says I'm excellent at coming up with ideas."

"Okay," said Nicola. "What's your idea?"

"Give me a *minute!*"

"Got it!" Sean snapped his fingers. "I'll rappel down into the castle from a helicopter late at night, with, like, a ski mask on, and dressed all in black, and I'll talk to you on the two-way radio and let you know how I'm going, and I'll just knock her out and toss her over my shoulder and then, ummmm, let's see . . .Who wants to take it from there?"

Shimlara said, "Don't forget the princess is a whole lot taller than you, Sean. You'd probably have trouble tossing her over your shoulder."

"You'd be surprised at what I can do." Sean cracked his knuckles and Shimlara snorted, unimpressed.

"Shimlara, did you say something about guards around the palace?" asked Tyler.

"Yep, lots of them," said Shimlara. "I don't want to sound negative, but you're all pretty small compared to the palace guards—even I am! They wouldn't think twice about shooting us if they caught us kidnapping the princess."

"Bulletproof vests." Sean pointed at his chest as if he wore a bulletproof vest to school every day.

"We've got to find an excuse to get her *out* of the palace," said Tyler.

"Okay, but how do we do that?" asked Greta. No one spoke.

"We could invite her to a party," suggested Katie tentatively. "Nicola says she's bored, so she might be happy to come."

"Like, a birthday party?" asked Shimlara. "I don't think she'd come to a commoner's birthday party. She would think it was beneath her."

"The party would have to be about *her*," said Greta. "It would have to be something that appealed to her ego."

"What about a Praise the Princess Pool Party?" asked Nicola. "We could have it right here in the backyard."

"Would she fall for it?" asked Tyler.

"I think she might," said Nicola. "We could say it's to pay tribute to her wonderful beauty and talent, blah, blah, blah."

"So we get her to the party," said Sean. "And then I rappel in through the roof . . ."

"Sean, I don't know if we're going to need any rappelling," said Nicola.

"Okay, so let's say we get her here to the pretend party," said Shimlara. "She'll probably bring at least one bodyguard with her."

"We'll have to distract the bodyguard, and then find a way to tie her up and tape up her mouth," said Nicola. "The problem is that if she screams, the bodyguard will come running."

"What if we hypnotized her?" said Katie. "My grandma does hypnosis—I think I could work out how to do it, at least for a few minutes. Then we could get her to tie *herself* up!"

"So we get her to the party, we distract the guard, we hypnotize her—then how do we get her to Earth?" asked Greta.

"We'll have to use Georgio's spaceship," said Nicola. "Do you think Plum would fly it for us, Shimlara? We could hide the princess so she wouldn't know we were doing anything illegal."

"I think so," said Shimlara. "She's pretty easygoing."

"Okay," said Nicola. "We've got a plan. Do you think it will work?"

She looked around the room.

They all shook their heads sadly.

"No."

"Not really."

"Probably not."

"Should we try it anyway?"

"Yes!"

"You bet!"

"Let's go for it!!"

Princess Petronella

IS CORDIALLY INVITED TO BE
GUEST OF HONOR AT A

PRAISE THE PRINCESS
POOL PARTY.

THIS REALLY FUN,
NOT-TO-BE-MISSED-OR-YOU-WILL-
REGRET-IT-FOR-THE-REST-OF-YOUR-LIFE
PHENOMENAL POOL PARTY
IS TO HONOR THE EXTRAORDINARY JOB
THE PRINCESS IS DOING WHILE HER PARENTS,
THE KING AND QUEEN, ARE AWAY ON VACATION.

AMAZING, RARE, AND UNUSUAL GIFTS
WILL BE PRESENTED TO THE PRINCESS.

THERE WILL ALSO BE SPEECHES
PRAISING THE PRINCESS FOR HER MANY
PRODIGIOUS TALENTS, HER INEFFABLE
BEAUTY, HER STUPENDOUS WIT, AND HER
GENERAL ALL-AROUND EMINENCE!

WHERE: 3087105804158 MADAGASKARAVARGERA DRIVE,
PARAGASKARVILLE
WHEN: TWO P.M., FRIDAY, JUNE 29

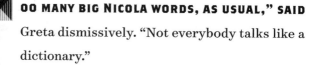

OO MANY BIG NICOLA WORDS, AS USUAL," SAID Greta dismissively. "Not everybody talks like a dictionary."

She handed back the invitation. Nicola had written the words and Shimlara had done the design on her computer. It was on a thick white scroll of paper with gold engraving and a red wax seal.

"I think it's a beautiful invitation," said Katie.

"She won't be able to resist," said Tyler.

"Okay," said Nicola. "So now we post the invitation—"

"Oh, NO!"

Everybody jumped as Shimlara clapped her hands over her face.

"What is it?" asked Tyler. "What's wrong?"

"I just remembered something Mom and Dad said when they sent their first petition to the princess about saving Earth."

"Ye-es?" encouraged Nicola.

"Well, they said the princess gets so much mail, it would be weeks before she would even see it."

"Can't we just take it ourselves and deliver it to her?" asked Tyler.

"Everybody tries that." Shimlara slumped down on her bed, looking despondent. "There are whole wheelbarrows of mail every day. I'm so sorry I didn't think of this earlier."

"Yes, you really should have thought of it," said Greta.

"No worries. We just ring up the princess and ask her to the party," said Sean.

"You can't just *ring up* the princess," said Shimlara. "She has servants to answer her phone. She would never talk to us."

"The best thing would be to deliver the invitation to her personally," said Tyler.

"But you need an appointment to see her," said Shimlara. "Dad made Nicola's appointment weeks before he'd even gone to Earth to pick the Ambassador."

"Oh," said Tyler.

Everybody sat silently, staring at the floor, trying to work out what to do.

Nicola glanced at her countdown watch. It said:

JUST A BIT OVER ONE DAY LEFT—
ALL YOUR CLEVER PLANS SHOULD BE COMING
TOGETHER NICELY BY NOW.

Grrrrr.

There was a slight rustle as a handwritten note slid under Shimlara's door. It was a note from Mully saying:

DO YOU WANT SOMETHING TO EAT OR DRINK?

Shimlara wrote on the bottom: YES, PLEASE!!! She slid it back under the door.

"That would be a good way to get the invitation to the princess," commented Katie. "If we could just slide it under her bedroom door."

"Why don't we just sneak in while she's sleeping and put it on her bedside table," said Greta in a sarcastic voice. "Be *realistic,* Katie."

"Actually," said Shimlara slowly, "maybe that's an option."

"Really?" said Nicola.

"Yep." Shimlara turned to Sean. "We might need you to do some rappelling after all."

21

I T WAS THE MIDDLE OF THE NIGHT. THE MEMBERS OF
the Space Brigade were dressed from head to toe in
black (or at least their darkest-colored clothes), with
black ski masks covering their faces.

Sean was so excited, Nicola thought he might
explode. Katie, on the other hand, was so nervous and pale,
Nicola was worried she might faint.

Georgio and Mully had gone to bed hours earlier,
leaving the Space Brigade asleep in sleep-pouches (Globagaskar's high-tech, softer, snugger version of sleeping
bags—they even had their own built-in thermostats so
you could adjust the temperature to suit) on Shimlara's
bedroom floor. Nicola had felt bad about telling them that
the Brigade wasn't taking any new action until the morning,
but Shimlara had said they'd understand once Earth was
saved.

Everyone reviewed multiplication tables in their heads
during dinner to make sure Georgio didn't read their minds
and work out what they were doing. He hadn't said anything except to remark that he'd always found the "one
times" table hardly worthy of reviewing, giving Sean a

pointed look, and that nine nines were not and never had been eighty-two, if anyone happened to be interested.

They had stayed awake for what seemed like ages until the house was still and quiet except for the sound of Georgio snoring. Then, they'd all crept on nervous tiptoes outside to the garage, where Shimlara apparently kept her very own helicopter, in the same way that most Earthling children would keep a bike.

"You've got a *helicopter*?" Tyler had said when Shimlara had mentioned this.

"Oh, yeah, I got one for my last birthday," said Shimlara. "Everyone in my class has got one. Most kids have got their own mini spaceships."

"And you're allowed to *fly* this helicopter?" Tyler was barely able to contain his envy.

"Of course!" Shimlara paused, then said honestly, "I'm not very good at it, though."

This was proving to be true.

They'd all crammed into the helicopter, with Shimlara behind the controls. Now they were flying to the Rainbow Palace to personally deliver the invitation to the princess. Sean would rappel down from the roof into the princess's bedroom and leave it sitting on her bedside table. Simple— as long as they made it to the palace without crashing.

The helicopter kept swooping down dangerously close

to the tops of buildings. With a cheerful "Oops-a-daisy!" Shimlara would pull on the controls and next thing they'd all be pinned to their seats as the helicopter shot straight up into the starry night sky.

"I think I'm going to be sick," moaned Katie.

"Are you going to be able to land the helicopter on the roof without knocking the palace down?" asked Greta.

"Who knows?!" Shimlara swung the controls violently to the left and Nicola's head knocked against the window.

"I see the palace!" said Tyler. He had a pair of binoculars pressed against the helicopter window. "Gosh. Is it made of . . . jewelry?"

"Precious stones," explained Nicola.

The palace looked even more beautiful at night. The rubies, emeralds, sapphires, and diamonds glittered mysteriously in the turquoise moonlight shining from Globagaskar's two moons.

"Okay," said Shimlara. "Time to go into Camouflage Mode. Can you pull that lever there, Sean?"

Sean pulled the lever and all of a sudden the noisy sounds of the helicopter blades vanished and the lights went off, plunging them into darkness and silence.

"None of the guards should be able to see or hear the helicopter now," whispered Shimlara. "Assuming we can trust the instruction book, of course. Some of the other features of the helicopter haven't actually worked that well."

"Oh great," muttered Greta.

"Ah, Shim, I think now might be a good time to land," said Sean. "That looks like a helicopter landing pad to me."

They were hovering over the very top of the castle and Nicola could see a large flat area with a circle marked on it.

"Okey-dokey," said Shimlara.

She did something with the pedals at her feet and the helicopter began to nosedive toward the helipad.

"Straighten up! Straighten up!" shouted Tyler.

"I don't want to die!" cried Greta. "I've got to finish my term as class president!"

"Greta, you're really starting to bug me." Shimlara did something else to the controls that caused the helicopter to veer crazily to the left as they hurtled down toward land.

"OUCH! OUCH! OUCH!" everybody said in unison as their heads banged against the side of the helicopter while it bounced along the helipad.

Finally it stopped bouncing and was still.

For a few seconds no one spoke as they all rubbed their heads.

Then Katie said, "Well done, Shimlara."

"Thank you," beamed Shimlara.

"Okay, let's get this show on the road." Sean opened the door of the helicopter and jumped lightly to the ground.

"Remember to stick to the plan!" ordered Nicola.

"Actually, I do have some suggestions about changing the plan," began Greta.

"Too late," said Nicola firmly.

The plan was that Tyler, Katie, and Greta would be the lookouts. They were to station themselves at different parts of the palace roof and keep an eye out for the guards. If they thought a guard was becoming suspicious, they would make a "meow" sound.

There had been a lot of arguments over this because Greta thought it would be preferable for the warning signal to be an owl's hoot. Sean suggested laughing like a hyena, but Nicola thought he was probably just throwing out that idea because he enjoyed arguing. In the end, the cat's meow had won.

In the meantime, Shimlara and Nicola would be responsible for operating the rope system that would lower Sean into the princess's bedroom so he could drop the invitation next to her bed, where it would be the first thing she saw when she woke up.

Hopefully she would assume it had been delivered by one of her ladies-in-waiting.

"Now we just need to find the princess's bedroom," said Shimlara. She pulled out the map she'd downloaded from the palace website and studied it carefully.

"Huh?" she said confusedly, turning it the other way around.

"Let me see," said Sean. "Everyone knows girls can't read maps."

He took the map from her. "Huh?" He twisted it around and brought it up close to his face and frowned. "Ummm. Okay. So right now we're ... ummmm, mmmm, let's see ..."

"Oh, for goodness sake." Greta snatched the map from him and examined it. She immediately looked up and pointed to a triangular vent on the far side of the roof next to a ruby-encrusted turret. "That vent over there is the top of the princess's bedroom."

"Good work!" said Nicola generously.

"Yes, well, that's why I should have been the Earthling Ambassador in the first place." Greta flounced off to her lookout point.

Sean, Shimlara, and Nicola went over to the vent and looked down at it apprehensively. Nicola put a finger to her lips, reminding them that the princess was asleep just beneath them.

Shimlara pulled Georgio's toolbox from her backpack and they each selected a screwdriver. Working quietly and efficiently, they unscrewed the corners of the vent's covering and lifted it off.

They gave one another quick thumbs-ups and got down

on their stomachs so they could peer into the opening.

At first Nicola couldn't see anything, but when her eyes adjusted to the darkness she could just make out the princess's four-poster bed and her head on a mound of pillows.

Gosh. She wore her diamond tiara even when she was sleeping.

There was a sudden loud rumbling noise and Nicola jumped back in fright.

"She snores just like Dad!" mouthed Shimlara, trying to suppress an attack of the giggles.

Sean was all businesslike. He strapped himself into his harness and tied the end of the rope firmly around a nearby emerald turret. He pushed his night-vision goggles over his eyes and whispered, "Ready."

Nicola silently handed him the invitation. Sean took it and held it between his teeth. *Great*, thought Nicola. *Now it will be all soggy and tooth-marked!*

Using both elbows for support, Sean lowered himself into the vent, while Nicola and Shimlara let out the safety rope. When he was far down enough, he flipped himself onto his stomach with his arms and legs spread out, so he was hanging above the princess's bed.

"Slowly!" whispered Nicola to Shimlara as they lowered him down. She didn't want Sean crashing onto the princess's floor.

Bit by bit they released the rope while Sean twirled in slow circles and the princess continued her rumbling snore.

Finally Sean was close enough to take the invitation from his mouth and place it on the bedside table.

"He's done it!" whispered Shimlara excitedly.

They began to haul on the rope to lift him back up, and Sean's elbow knocked against the side of the princess's chest of drawers.

The princess woke with a start. She sat straight up in bed. "Who are you?" She rubbed her eyes. "And just WHAT are you doing in my bedroom?"

ICOLA AND SHIMLARA FROZE. THEIR EYES
locked in mutual terror. Nicola's heart did a
triple somersault. Shimlara's eyes were as wide
as saucers.

Somewhere in the distance, a cat meowed.

They heard Sean speaking in the room beneath them,
his voice shaky and polite. "Okay, just relax, ah, Princess,
and go back to sleep. You're dreaming. This is all just a
weird, far-out dream."

"I am NOT dreaming! I'm wide awake!" Princess
Petronella threw back the covers of her bed to reveal an all-
in-one yellow pajama suit. "I demand to know what you're
doing here. Are you trying to *rob* me, you horrible boy? I'll
have you beheaded!"

"Ah, Nic . . . boss?" said Sean without looking up. "What
would you like me to do here?"

The princess peered around suspiciously and then
tilted her head toward the vent and caught sight of Nicola.
"I know you! You're that whiny Earthling!"

"Oh dear," said Nicola. Another cat meowed somewhere. Was the palace overrun with cats?

"Look, calm down, we're just trying to invite you to a party," said Sean.

"I don't believe you. Nobody likes me. I never get invited to parties. Are you trying to kidnap me? Is that it?" demanded the princess.

Now there seemed to be a whole chorus of louder and louder meows.

"It's not real cats—it's the signal!" said Shimlara. "The guards must have seen us!"

"I don't like boys." The princess shook her finger fiercely at Sean, who was still spinning over her bed. "You know what? I think I might have you tortured for a few weeks before I have your head sliced off!"

Sean's legs and arms spun wildly in different directions. "Nicola! Get me out of here!"

Glancing up, Nicola saw Tyler, Greta, and Katie all running toward them, shouting, "MEOW! ONE OF THE GUARDS ON THE GROUND SAW US! MEOW, MEOW!"

A bright yellow spotlight swept back and forth across the palace roof. Nicola made her decision.

"Grab her!" she called to Sean. "We're kidnapping her NOW!"

Sean didn't hesitate. He kicked his legs off the side of the princess's bedroom wall, swung hard toward her, and threw his arms around her waist. "GOT HER!"

The princess easily tore herself away from him. "You have NOT got me!"

"He's too short," said Shimlara desperately. "He'll never do it."

Sean made another grab for the princess, and this time the point in her tiara snagged itself in Sean's black sweater as she tried to wriggle away.

"OWWWW!" She twisted her head from side to side, but the tiara only got more tangled. Sean threw his arms and legs around the princess's back like a koala clinging to a tree.

"Okay, I've SORT of got her!" he yelled.

Nicola and Shimlara pulled on the rope, nearly falling over backward with the combined weight of the princess and Sean. Tyler, Greta, and Katie ran up and snatched the rope to help them pull.

The princess kicked and screamed like a wild animal and sunk her teeth into Sean's hand. "Augggh! Faster, faster!" screamed Sean.

"I don't remember this being part of the plan, Nicola!" shouted Greta.

"Oh, would you please SHUT UP, Greta!" Katie shouted back. Then she immediately felt guilty and said, "Please?"

The Space Brigade gave a final wrench on the ropes, and Sean and the princess tumbled out of the vent and onto the palace roof like two grappling football players. The princess's tiara was jerked free of Sean's sweater, leaving a gaping hole.

"GUARDS!" hollered the princess, scrambling to her feet and straightening her tiara. "I am being KIDNAPPED by disgusting, squidgy little Earthlings and one dreadful commoner!"

"Quickly! We need to tie her up and carry her to the helicopter!" ordered Nicola.

"GUARDS, you incompetent nincompoops! I order you to come and save me RIGHT NOW!"

Everybody tried their best to tie up the princess, running around her in circles as she swatted at them like flies and jumped up and down on the spot.

"Keep still!" cried Shimlara in frustration.

"Why should I keep still? You're trying to KIDNAP me!"

"Hypnotize her, Katie!" said Sean.

Looking terrified, Katie pulled off her necklace and began swinging it slowly back and forth. "Ummm . . . watch the necklace, please. Okay, now you're beginning to feel very sleepy."

The princess grimaced down at her. "I am NOT feeling sleepy, you tiny twerp! I am very awake and very ANGRY! *Gshe-ghd-ash!*"

Greta had pulled a roll of masking tape from her backpack, ripped off a piece, jumped up on top of an emerald tower, and stuck the tape firmly over the princess's mouth.

"Good one, Greta," said Sean.

The princess's eyes bulged.

"Got her hands!" said Tyler. He'd managed to tie the princess's hands together behind her back.

"Okay, let's get her to the helicopter," said Nicola. They surrounded the princess and began pushing, shoving, and pulling her toward the helicopter. It was hard work because she was so much taller than all of them, apart from Shimlara. The princess didn't help matters by deciding on a new strategy of becoming limp and heavy like a bag of potatoes.

"We need to get her to move faster," said Sean. "Look."

They looked up to see dozens of helicopters circling above them.

"Lay down your weapons!" boomed a fierce voice.

"Ha ha! We can't—we don't have any!" Shimlara yelled back.

"No need to mention that," said Tyler.

Sean sighed. "I *knew* we should have brought weaponry."

They redoubled their efforts, frantically pushing the princess toward the helicopter.

"I wonder if she's ticklish," said Tyler.

Nicola looked up at the princess and caught a tiny spark of fear in her eyes.

"TICKLE HER!" she shouted.

Everybody obeyed and the princess tried desperately to escape from all the tickling fingers. She ducked and weaved as if she were trying to win a dance competition.

"Tickle HARDER!" shouted Nicola. "Go get the helicopter started, Shimlara!"

Shimlara ran off, while Nicola, Tyler, Sean, Katie, and Greta vigorously tickled the princess. In her panic to evade their tickling, the princess actually *ran* straight to Shimlara's helicopter and threw herself in the door. The rest of them tumbled in behind her and Nicola shouted, "GO, GO, GO!" just as the first guard ran across the palace roof and grabbed hold of Greta's foot.

HE HELICOPTER TOOK OFF STRAIGHT AND SMOOTH
into the dark sky. Below them they could see the
guard holding Greta's school shoe, shaking his fist
ferociously.

"He's got my shoe!" said Greta as if that were
the most important thing to worry about at the moment. The
guard tossed the shoe away and Greta yelled, "Excuse *me*!
That shoe is part of the Honeyville Primary School uniform!"

"Shgished ugggh idddy Ed Ed Ed!" The princess was
making strange garbled sounds through her taped-up
mouth.

"What do you think she's saying?" asked Katie.

"I think she's talking about how she's going to have all
our heads cut off," said Sean.

"Oh great," said Katie.

Tyler had his face pressed to the back window of the
helicopter. "They're chasing us!" he cried as dozens of helicopters with revolving red lights and shrieking sirens filled
the sky around them.

Sean pulled the Camouflage Mode lever again. "Now
they can't see us. Ha!"

"Mmmm," said Shimlara. "Did I mention Camouflage Mode only works for five minutes at a time?"

"Ho!" mumbled the princess. Her eyes were triumphant above the masking tape.

The helicopter filled with red light as one of the guards' helicopters flew dangerously close to them.

"Can you fly faster?" asked Nicola.

"Well . . ." Shimlara scratched her cheek nervously. "We could go to Super-Fast Mode, but the instruction book does warn against trying it until you're a very advanced flyer. I mean, I guess I'm getting *pretty* good at it—oopsie! Sorry, everybody!"

"Don't you even *think* about flying in Super-Fast Mode!" Greta rubbed her elbow crossly. "You'll kill us all!"

"But the guards will kill us all if we don't get away," Tyler pointed out.

"Yeah, I'd rather Shimlara killed us," said Sean.

"Actually, I think Shimlara's flying is improving all the time," said Katie.

"It's your decision, Nicola," said Shimlara.

"Ummmm . . ." Nicola's head ached from all this difficult decision-making.

Tyler looked at his watch. "We've got two minutes of Camouflage Mode left."

Sean's hand hovered over the lever marked SUPER-FAST.

"Nic? Should I do it?"

Nicola looked out the window at one of the helicopters passing by. The guard sitting in the passenger seat was punching a black-gloved fist into the palm of his hand over and over. He looked like he was preparing to punch an Earthling.

"Yes. Do it," said Nicola.

"You ready, Shim?" asked Sean.

"As ready as I'll ever be!"

Greta said, "This is the stupidest—"

Sean pulled the lever and the helicopter shot forward so fast that Shimlara's hands were thrown from the controls.

What have I done? Nicola thought. All she could see through the window was a blurry streak of colors as they hurtled through the sky.

"It's okay!" Shimlara clutched the controls. "I've got it all under—" And suddenly the helicopter flipped over and everyone was shouting and screaming as they dangled upside down, held on only by their seat belts.

"DON'T WORRY!" yelled Shimlara, and to Nicola's surprise, she heard Katie laugh crazily.

With a jolt the helicopter tipped the right way up and they continued to zoom across the skyline.

"Okay, everybody, JUST HANG ON! We're coming in to land!"

Nicola gripped the sides of her seat. The helicopter nosedived toward the ground. They were all going to die and it would be Nicola's fault.

"THIS IS ALL YOUR FAULT, NICOLA!" yelled Greta.

"ISH MISH GFUG GLIG, GLIG, GLIG!" That was the princess.

"WHOOOOEEE!" cried Sean.

"YOU'RE DOING A GREAT JOB, SHIMLARA!" screamed Katie.

"SWITCH BACK TO NORMAL SPEED!" cried Tyler.

CRASH!

BANG!

SMASH!

And then there was silence.

ICOLA OPENED HER EYES. HER SHOULDER
ached and she thought her knee might be
bleeding, but otherwise she was definitely still
alive.

"Is everybody alive?" she demanded.

"I am," said Sean.

"So am I," said Tyler.

"Me too," said Katie.

"I'm fine," said Shimlara. "Although my arm sort of
hurts."

"No thanks to you, but yes, I'm alive," said Greta.

"Ishgo mishgo ed!" said the princess.

"Where have we landed?" asked Nicola.

"WHAT IN THE GALAXY IS GOING ON HERE?"

It was Georgio's voice. Nicola could see him marching
toward the helicopter. His hair was all mussed up and he
was wearing bright green pajamas. Pajamas were so funny
on Globagaskar. Georgio looked like a gigantic baby with
a mustache.

"I think we might have landed right on top of Dad's
aero-car." Shimlara pressed a button to lift the dome of

the helicopter. She was holding her right arm at a strange angle. "Hi, Dad."

"Don't you 'Hi, Dad' me! It's the MIDDLE OF THE NIGHT! I was sound asleep enjoying a particularly pleasant dream, when I heard this terrific bang on the driveway. We nearly jumped out of our skins!"

"I'm sorry, Georgio," said Nicola. "It wasn't meant to work out this way. Things just got out of hand."

Mully appeared behind Georgio, rubbing her eyes. Her pajamas were bright pink.

"Is everybody all right?" she asked. "I thought you were all sleeping nice and snug in your sleep-pouches! Nicola, your parents are going to be so angry with me. Shimlara, what have you done to your arm? It looks—OH MY STARS AND MOONS! Georgio, over there, it's—"

With one hand over her mouth, she nudged Georgio and pointed wordlessly at Princess Petronella sitting between Sean and Greta.

Georgio was still busy checking out the damage to his aero-car. "I mean, Bounce-a-Guard can only do so much," he muttered as he squatted down and ran a finger across the paintwork. "It wasn't designed to have a helicopter full of wicked children landing smack-bang on top of it!"

"Georgio!" Mully tugged at the back of Georgio's pajamas and he stood up.

"What is it?" he said irritably.

Then he caught sight of Princess Petronella.

"Your Royal Highness," he said respectfully, bowing deeply. "I'm so sorry, I didn't realize you were along for the ride. Of course, if it was *your* decision to land smack-bang on my aero-car—"

"Ah, Georgio," said Mully quietly. "I don't think it was her decision to be here at all."

Finally Georgio seemed to notice that the princess had her hands tied behind her back and masking tape over her mouth.

"Ish mgish ed, ed, ed!" The princess's eyes blazed.

Georgio gulped and looked at Nicola. "You don't mean you've actually kidnapped Princess Petronella?"

"I tried to tell her it was a stupid idea!" said Greta. "Do you think I should take over as Earthling Ambassador now?"

"Oh, *do* be quiet, you dreadful child." Georgio tried to smooth down his messed-up hair.

"The plan was to take the princess to Earth," explained Nicola. "I wanted her to see how beautiful it was—I thought that might change her mind about turning it into a garbage can."

Georgio's voice was clear and precise in Nicola's head: *This is risky because no doubt the princess is trying to read as many of our minds as she can, so I'll talk fast. Hopefully at least some of her attention is on trying to breathe through the gag, and that will distract her from what I'm about to say, which is that taking her to Earth isn't a bad idea. But I just need to work out the right things to say here. Obviously I can't be seen supporting your kidnapping her.* Aloud he said, "But *kidnapping* her! I'm sure if you had humbly asked the princess, she would have been delighted to accompany you!"

The princess shook her head vigorously.

"How were you planning to get to Earth?" asked Mully.

"We were going to ask Plum to fly us in Dad's spaceship," said Shimlara.

"Well, the only tiny glitch in your plans is that Plum has borrowed my spaceship to go on a romantic intergalactic date with her boyfriend," said Georgio. "Apparently I had to make up for spoiling her birthday."

"Eeedghghhhhh!" exclaimed the princess.

"Yes, indeed, Your Highness," said Georgio. "I do understand you're in a hurry to get to Earth so you can make your final decision! We just need to work out your transport."

"Gshhh issssh ridgy didge!" The princess shook her head about maniacally.

"Is that tiara *superglued* to her head?" asked Sean.

Georgio nodded graciously as if he were at a tea party

with the princess. "Yes, of course, it must seem highly unusual. However, let me assure you this is certainly *not* a kidnapping as it might appear, but simply an overly enthusiastic attempt by these sweet young Earthlings to introduce you to their planet! The tape across your mouth and the ropes are ... ummm, an ancient Earthling custom symbolizing, erm, RESPECT! They simply indicate the fact that you don't need to say or do a thing! You can just sit back and relax because the whole trip is in their hands! Admittedly their hands are somewhat incompetent at times, but their planet is so charmingly backward that we can hardly hold that against them, now can we? Of course, if, after inspecting Earth, you still decide to destroy it, I'm sure these dear little Earthlings will be perfectly happy to accept your decision!"

"Huh?" said Sean. But he shut up when Greta elbowed him hard in the side.

The princess bounced up and down in frustration.

"OGALOG!"

"Yes, yes, Princess Petronella, I know you're growing impatient," soothed Georgio. "I just can't quite think—"

Mully spoke up. "I have an idea," she said.

25

I THINK WE SHOULD GIVE SHIMLARA HER CHRISTMAS present a bit early this year," said Mully.

"Oh, no, don't ruin the surprise for her," said Katie.

"It's okay if it's important for the mission," said Shimlara nobly.

It turned out that Shimlara's Christmas present was a Mini Easy-Ride spaceship.

Tyler was flabbergasted. "You were getting a *spaceship* as a Christmas present. A *spaceship*!"

"Your father and I are too big to fit into a mini spaceship," said Mully. "Otherwise we'd fly it back to Earth for you, considering the recent demonstration of your piloting skills. But desperate times call for desperate measures. And you've flown your friends' spaceships a few times, haven't you, darling?"

"Yes," said Shimlara, but she looked tense and unhappy. "The only thing is—I think I've done something bad to my arm."

"Oh, *Shimlara*," said Mully, in exactly the same way Nicola's mom said, "Oh, *Nicola*," whenever she hurt herself. She gently examined Shimlara's arm, shaking her head. "I think you might have broken it. We'll have to get an instant cast on it right away. Well, you're in no condition to fly—one of the others will have to do it. Which member of the Space Brigade do you recommend, Nicola?"

That was easy.

"Tyler," said Nicola instantly.

"Hmmmph," said Greta. "Talk about favoritism."

"Although notice she doesn't favor her loving older brother," said Sean.

Tyler stood soldier-straight, his eyes glittering and the tips of his ears—always a giveaway—glowing pink. "I'll give it a go," he said.

"Of course, it is a *mini* spaceship," said Georgio. "So it's very slow. It will take you five long, boring minutes to get to Earth, but the advantage is that it's very easy to operate—or so the brochures say!"

"Fortunately, the palace guards are not the most intelligent creatures," said Mully. "So that should buy you a little time. And it's lucky Earth is such a large, populated planet. Tracking you down will be like looking for a needle in a haystack."

"Sean left the invitation to the pool party in the princess's bedroom," pointed out Greta. "If someone finds it, the guards will be heading straight to this address right now."

"HA!" said the princess through her taped-up mouth.

"I can feel the most terrible migraine coming on," said Georgio.

"Nicola, you need to get your people off this planet *right away*." Mully spoke in a rapid, deadly serious tone of voice Nicola had never heard her use before. "Georgio, take Tyler to the spaceship and start going through the instruction manual with him. Katie, go with Shimlara and she'll show you where to find the first-aid kit. I'll be there to help you with the cast in just a moment. Greta, you can collect everybody's luggage. Sean, help the princess—*gently!*—along to the garage. Nicola, come with me into my study. I need to have a very quick chat with you."

For a few seconds everybody stared in wonder at this new Mully. Even though she was still dressed in her funny pink pajamas, she seemed to be an entirely different sort of person.

"Mully was an officer in the Globagaskar Army when we first met," explained Georgio. He beamed proudly at his wife. "Isn't she *impressive*?"

"MOVE IT, MOVE IT!" barked Mully, and everybody hurried to obey her.

Nicola followed Mully into her study.

As she shut the door, Mully turned back into a normal mom. "Is that knee hurting you too much, dear?"

Nicola looked down at her grazed knee. "No, it's fine."

"I want to give you something," said Mully. "During my army days, I was in charge of weapons purchasing for a while, and the weapon manufacturers keep sending me free samples, in spite of all the letters I send telling them to take me off their mailing lists. I think this particular weapon might come in handy."

Mully pulled a silver briefcase from underneath her desk and placed it in front of Nicola. It had a round lock, like on a safe.

"The code is 55-77-99." Mully swiftly twisted the dial. "Don't tell anybody else the code. I don't want anyone making the decision to use these weapons except you, Nicola."

The lock clicked open and Mully lifted the lid. Nicola peered in, preparing herself not to flinch if she saw something horrible and scary, like guns or knives.

"Oh!" she said in surprise.

The case held a set of what looked like colorful tennis balls. They didn't look at all dangerous.

"They're freeze-grenades," explained Mully. She lifted one of the balls out of the case and showed it to Nicola. "They're extremely effective weapons. I've set them especially for use against the palace guards. If you throw one at any guard within a five-meter radius, he or she will be frozen solid for ten minutes, giving you plenty of time to escape. Being frozen by a freeze-grenade is *not* a pleasant experience. It feels extremely cold and once the thawing begins, very itchy. By the time one can move again, one tends to be extremely upset and angry. So if the guards catch up with you on Earth, my advice is to throw the freeze-grenades, dump the princess, and run for your lives."

"Right." Nicola nodded, trying to look like a cool-headed army major, as if the words "run for your lives" didn't fill her with jelly-knee terror.

"Remember, the grenades are for emergency use only against the guards," said Mully. "I recommend you do not tell your brother Sean about these, for obvious reasons."

"He'd love to try them," agreed Nicola.

"Well, I just hope you don't need them," said Mully. "But I'll feel safer if I know you're armed in some way. Got all that?"

"Got it," swallowed Nicola.

Mully snapped the case closed. "Don't forget. The code is 55-77-99. You won't forget it, will you?"

"55-77-99," repeated Nicola. "I won't forget."

"Georgio and I will be doing our best to stall the palace guards on Globagaskar for as long as we can," said Mully. "We have it all worked out. We'll make it look like we have the princess in the aero-car. I'm going to call Molly Smith from the Save the Little Earthlings Committee. She has a daughter with red, curly hair just like the princess who fancies herself as an actress. We'll make a show of dragging her to the aero-car and taking off. Fortunately, I did aero-speed-driving as part of my army training, so I should be able to give them a run for their money before they realize they've been duped and come looking for you."

Nicola was slightly in awe. To think she'd thought Mully was just an ordinary mom. Then again, maybe all ordinary moms revealed unexpected talents in times of crisis.

"Listen to me, Nicola," continued Mully. Her voice was grave, her eyes flat and serious. "Kidnapping the princess is a very serious crime. If she chooses, she could have all of you thrown in jail."

"She's threatened to have us beheaded." Nicola hoped Mully would laugh in an "as if!" way, but she just looked more serious.

"Well, she could do that, too, if she wanted," said Mully. "Georgio and I would also be punished for helping you— and so would all the other members of the Save the Little Earthlings Committee. So if you want to save your planet and all our lives, it's absolutely essential that you do one thing. It's the one thing I always hoped you'd achieve. It's the one thing I think will give us success."

Nicola's fingers tightened around the handle of the briefcase.

"What's that?"

Mully bent all the way down from her huge height so she was at the same level as Nicola and could look her straight in the eyes.

"You must become friends with the princess."

26

**ELCOME ABOARD, ESTEEMED PASSENGERS!**
My name is Tyler Brown and I'll be your
captain for today's journey." Tyler's voice
was crackly and nervous over the spaceship's loudspeakers.

"Ah, Tyler, maybe we could skip that part," suggested Nicola. Outside the spaceship she could see Mully
and Georgio standing just to the side of the launch pad,
looking anxious. Mully tapped her finger meaningfully on
her watch.

Nicola said, "We're in a bit of a hurry."

"Georgio told me to follow everything *exactly* as it's
written in the instruction booklet," said Tyler.

"Oh, all right," said Nicola. "Just as fast as you can."
She didn't want to make him any more nervous than he
already was.

She looked around the tiny spaceship, which was a
miniature, prettier version of Georgio's. Everybody was
strapped tightly into their passenger-pods. They each
had at least one Band-Aid on a nasty cut or graze. Shimlara's arm was in a cast, supported by a sling. Everyone

looked grim and quiet. Even the princess had stopped trying to talk and was resting her head against the spaceship wall, her eyes closed, her tiara still in place. Nicola wondered what she was thinking. It was going to be hard to become friends with her. Even Greta seemed like a friendly, easygoing person compared to Princess Petronella.

"Right." Tyler squinted at the computer in front of him and began to type something slowly and painstakingly. "My destination planet is . . . Earth."

He turned around to Nicola.

"Where exactly on Earth should we go?"

Nicola could hear a clattering sound of approaching helicopters in the distance. Someone must have found the invitation. The guards were on their way.

"Um, just put Australia," she said hurriedly.

"A-u-s . . ." Tyler punched in the letters one by one.

"HURRY UP!" exploded Greta.

"Leave him alone," said Shimlara. "He's never done this before."

"Esteemed passengers, please fasten your seat belts and prepare for blastoff," said Tyler into the microphone.

Nicola glanced out the spaceship window and saw Georgio leaping about like a furious orangutan and mouthing the words, "GO, GO!"

"Tyler," said Nicola. "This is a direct order. I'm ordering you to blast off NOW."

"Yes, *sir*!" said Tyler, and he banged one fist hard on a large red button.

There was a roaring sound and the spaceship filled with orange light. Outside, Mully and Georgio shielded their faces from the heat of the flames.

The spaceship quivered, as if it wasn't certain what to do next.

"Mmmm." Tyler scratched his head.

Suddenly they blasted straight into the night air through the garage roof, which was now flipped up and open. (Luckily Shimlara had remembered to press the button marked SPACESHIP ROOF EXIT.)

"WHOOOEEEE!" yelled Sean.

All around them was silent velvety blackness and the silver glow of starlight.

"Look! There's Globagaskar!" Shimlara pointed down at what looked like a golf ball disappearing in the distance.

The princess made a squeaking sound through her taped mouth.

"Maybe we should take her tape off so she can talk now," suggested Katie.

Nicola began to speak, but Tyler interrupted her. "Esteemed passengers, please prepare for—"

It was like the spaceship had just slid over the very highest point of a roller coaster. They plunged down so fast that the air rushed out of Nicola's lungs.

I don't even like roller coasters, thought Nicola. She closed her eyes and waited for the huge crash that was sure to follow and would probably hurt.

". . . landing," said Tyler calmly.

Nicola opened her eyes. "What happened?"

"We're here," said Tyler.

"But there wasn't even a bang," said Katie.

"Yep, I got it under control at the last second," said Tyler modestly. "Sorry about the nosedive. Won't happen again."

"Tyler, you're a *natural!*" said Shimlara.

Tyler blushed pink. "I don't know about that."

"It was very quick," said Nicola. "It seemed faster than five minutes."

Sean unbuckled his belt and clapped Tyler on the shoulder. "Good one, Tyler. So, whereabouts on Earth have we landed?"

He pulled the lever on the spaceship door and looked out.

"What's that awful *smell*?" Greta wrinkled her nose. A strange, horrible smell filled the spaceship. It was a mixture of dried out seaweed, Nicola's dad's tennis shoes, and old cat-food tins.

Nicola unbuckled her seat belt and went to peer over Sean's shoulder.

"All I can see is ... mud." She held her nose. "Bubbling ... black ... mud."

They weren't going to have much luck convincing the princess to save Earth if this was all they could show her. Besides the smell, the sky was a menacing dirty yellow and there wasn't a tree or bird in sight, let alone a butterfly. The mud stretched as far as she could see. It was like they'd landed on a huge mud desert.

"Hopefully we can catch a bus to somewhere nicer," she said to Sean.

"Yeah, but I don't exactly see any bus stops." Sean took off his baseball cap and scratched the top of his head.

Shimlara appeared behind them. "Is this Earth? It doesn't look like I thought it would look. Actually it reminds me of something we studied in intergalactic geography. Now what was it?"

Just then Nicola saw a figure in the distance coming toward them. It looked like a rather plump woman carrying an umbrella.

"Oh good," she said. "We can ask that lady about the nearest bus stop."

"I'll go." Sean jumped out of the spaceship. There was a glooping sound as he sank up to his knees in the black mud.

"Huh!" said Sean, in a pleased way, as if he enjoyed being knee-deep in mud. He began wading his way toward the lady with the umbrella.

Nicola turned back around to find the princess having some sort of fit. She was wriggling around in her seat, bobbing her head up and down, and rolling her eyes like a frightened horse.

"I guess you'd better take the masking tape off now," said Nicola to Katie. "Let's hear what she has to say. As long as her hands stay tied for now."

Katie was nervous as she reached over and tugged gently at the edge of the tape. "This might hurt a little, Princess Petronella."

"Oh for heaven's sake," said Greta, and she ripped the tape from the princess's mouth in one swift movement.

"We're not on Earth, you ridiculous fools," Princess Petronella spat out. "We're on ARTH!"

At the word "Arth," Shimlara gasped.

"And that's NOT a *lady* your brother is so cheerily waving at," continued the princess. "It's an *Arth-Creature* looking forward to a delicious Earthling snack!"

HE'S RIGHT." SHIMLARA SPOKE SO FAST AND breathlessly, she could barely get the words out. "Our teacher showed us pictures. That's why it looks familiar. Arth is at the top of the Galaxy's Ten Most Dangerous Planets list. Arth-Creatures eat ALL other species—Globagaskarians, Earthlings, whatever!"

"I mustn't have pressed the *E* key hard enough." Tyler sounded devastated. "I should have been more careful."

"You were rushing," said Katie. "It could have happened to anyone."

"So are you just going to sit around and have a good long chat about it?" asked Princess Petronella. "May I suggest we get out of here, *fast*?"

"SEAN!" yelled Nicola. "COME BACK RIGHT NOW!"

Sean didn't seem to hear. He kept wading through the mud toward the creature, waving his arm to get its attention. Either he was too far away to hear Nicola, or he was just pretending not to hear her, which was something he often did when it suited him.

"Nic-o-la."

It was such a croaky, quivery voice and it sounded so unlike Greta that it took Nicola a confused moment to identify the voice. Greta's face was chalky white. "Look." She pointed a shaky finger to the left of Sean and the lady.

Nicola felt a jolt of pure fear. A line of squat furry brown creatures with large umbrella-shaped heads, curved, cruel claws, and hungry, sharp-toothed mouths came lumbering toward Sean.

Nicola could hear a strange low humming sound becoming louder and louder.

"They're smacking their lips," explained Princess Petronella.

"Right," said Shimlara. "Let's go rescue Sean."

"Wait!" Nicola grabbed her by the elbow just before she launched herself from the spaceship. "We need to arm ourselves."

She pulled the silver case Mully had given her from underneath the seat. She never expected that she would have to use it.

"Untie the princess," she told Greta. "She can help us."

"Do you really think it's wise to be untying our *prisoner*?" asked Greta, but she was already starting to untie the ropes around the princess's hands.

"I'm going to give you each a freeze-grenade," said

Nicola. "We'll have to surround the Arth-Creatures to make sure we get every single one of them."

"Quick!" Tyler took another look out the spaceship window. "They're getting closer."

Nicola twisted the first dial to 55.

But what were the other two numbers? Her mind was like a blank sheet of paper.

"Hurry!' cried Shimlara.

"55-77-99," snapped Greta.

Nicola stared at her.

"Mully told me to remember those numbers just in case you needed them," said Greta. "She said that they were important, but she didn't tell me what they were for."

"Thank you," said Nicola.

"Lucky some of us have got good memories," huffed Greta.

Nicola twisted the dials and opened the case, handing a freeze-grenade to each person in the spaceship, including the princess.

"Just throw them as close as you can to the creatures. When they hit the ground and explode, they give off a cloud of gas that will freeze anything within a five-meter radius."

"*I* know how to use a freeze-grenade," said the princess haughtily. "Although I don't see why I should help save the lives of my kidnappers."

Nicola looked at Shimlara's injured arm. "Can you throw with your left hand? Maybe you should stay here in the spaceship."

Shimlara grabbed a grenade with her left hand. "I can do it."

"NICOLAAAAAAAAAA!" It was Sean yelling.

"We're coming. Just stand still!" Nicola poked her head out of the spaceship.

"Okay." She looked back at the other members of the Space Brigade. "We've got to spread out and surround them. Don't throw your grenade until you're in a position where you can get as many Arth-Creatures as possible. If we don't get all of them and we haven't got any grenades left then we're—"

"Lunch," finished the princess, smiling grimly. "They'll be having us for lunch."

28

HE MEMBERS OF THE SPACE BRIGADE—MINUS
Sean—stood crowded together in the small space-
ship cabin, clutching their freeze-grenades and
looking expectantly at Nicola.

"Let's go, everybody!" she ordered, trying to
sound confident instead of terrified.

Her eyes watered as she stepped onto the steps of the
aircraft and the horrible stench filled her nostrils. She realized that they'd actually landed on the outer edge of what
appeared to be a gigantic, scooped-out crater. It was like
an Olympic stadium, except the steep sides were lined with
boulders instead of seats, and the middle was a vast prairie
of black, bubbling mud.

Right in the middle of the crater was a heart-stopping
sight. At least twenty Arth-Creatures were purposefully
plodding through the mud from all directions, forming a
big, uneven circle around Sean. He had turned his baseball
cap around backward and was bending at the knees, his
arms crossed in kung fu attack position. Only Sean would
think he could single-handedly take on a pack of dangerous
alien creatures, after three beginner kung fu lessons.

Nicola clamped her mouth shut to stop herself from screaming for her mom and dad. This wasn't a bad dream. It was real. Her brother could be torn to bloody shreds and eaten in front of her. She needed to *think*. If the Space Brigade was going to make it out of this alive, they needed to be smarter than the Arth-Creatures.

With quivering legs she walked clumsily down the spaceship stairway, tightly holding her freeze-grenade.

"Quick!" she shouted to the others as they followed her down the steps. "We need to be close enough to throw our grenades, but not so close they can come after us. Luckily it doesn't look like they move very fast."

"What if I don't throw it straight?" Katie held her grenade cupped in both hands as if it might explode at any second. "You know how hopeless I am at softball."

"You'll be fine." Nicola tried not to think about Katie's habit of letting the softball slip straight through her fingers. The nasty girls called her Butterfingers.

"Just concentrate on what you're doing for once, Butterfingers," said Greta.

"Ignore her," said Nicola to Katie. "You can do it. Come on! Split up, everybody!"

Mud flew, splattering everybody's clothes and faces as they tried to run, slipping and sliding and clutching their grenades.

"Stick to the sides. It's drier!" advised Tyler.

With their longer legs, Shimlara and the princess led the way. Greta and Tyler followed Shimlara to the left, while Katie and Nicola followed the princess, who had shot off like a bullet from a gun, to the right.

Was the princess trying to escape? Everything was happening so quickly, Nicola didn't even know where to direct her attention first.

"Take *that*!" she heard Shimlara shout.

Without stopping, Nicola looked back over her shoulder to see Shimlara throw her freeze-grenade from the far-left-hand side of the crater. It soared high in the yellow sky, hit the mud, and exploded with a billowing cloud of purple smoke.

The smoke cleared to reveal a group of Arth-Creatures blinking and turning their massive heads this way and that. Their lip-smacking sounds became a low, spine-chilling growl. No longer were they out to dine on a leisurely lunch. Now they were really, really *mad*. The freeze-grenades didn't seem to be working.

Shimlara slowly, cautiously tried to back away up the side of the crater. Her sling was muddy. She held her good hand out, like a policeman saying "stop." Nicola skidded to a halt. Now what? Were the freeze-grenades broken? Had she misunderstood Mully's instructions? *We're all going to die*, she thought.

Suddenly she remembered Mully saying, "I've set them aside especially for use against the palace guards."

With trembling hands, Nicola turned over the grenade and noticed a small control panel on the back with instructions in small red letters. It said:

THIS FREEZE-GRENADE CURRENTLY SET
FOR ONE (1) USE AGAINST:

Bossy, bad-tempered types, e.g. palace guards,
large policemen, etc.

Furious family members, e.g. brothers, sisters, fathers—
WARNING: WILL NOT FREEZE MOTHERS

Dangerous Earth animals, e.g. tigers, lions,
hippos, spiders, etc.

Hungry Arth-Creatures

Miscellaneous

There was a movable arrow on the side pointing at "Bossy, bad-tempered types." Quickly, Nicola slid it down to "Hungry Arth-Creatures." She looked up to see who was the closest person to help Shimlara. It was Tyler, lurching gamely along, his arms flailing. His glasses were caked with mud. He was probably half blind.

"Tyler!" she yelled. "You need to change your grenade setting to Arth-Creatures! There's a control panel on the back!"

Luckily Tyler was good with anything mechanical.

The Arth-Creatures Shimlara had tried to freeze were pawing the ground like angry bulls. Suddenly they charged straight for her. Shimlara screamed.

"Now!" shouted Nicola.

Like a good soldier, Tyler obeyed instantly. He threw his grenade at the front of the pack charging at Shimlara. It hit one of the Arth-Creatures in the back of the head and exploded.

The smoke cleared and Nicola watched with a pounding heart.

YES! This time it had worked. About ten Arth-Creatures were frozen, their claws up, their huge mouths agape, as if someone had pressed a pause button.

"Awesome!" shouted Sean from the middle of the crater. The Arth-Creatures who had been charging behind crashed into the frozen ones and tumbled to the ground. They nosed and pawed at their frozen friends before climbing to their feet, stomping the ground, and fixing furious eyes on Tyler.

"Everybody change the settings on your grenades!" called out Nicola.

"Run, Tyler!" cried Shimlara.

Tyler smeared his fingers across his muddy glasses and staggered one way and then the other, like he was balancing on a seesaw.

"They're going to get him!" screamed Katie. Nicola

squinted, trying to see through the smoke. Greta was in the best position to help Tyler.

"Greta, grenade, *now!*"

"Calm down, I've got it all under control!" Greta fiddled with the setting on the back of her grenade. Suddenly it slipped straight through her muddy fingers and exploded directly in front of her. Greta froze on the spot, with her fingers outstretched and her face a mask of frantic horror at her mistake. Obviously she hadn't managed to change the setting from "Bossy, bad-tempered types."

Three Arth-Creatures were now just the length of a supermarket aisle away from Tyler.

"Ohhhhhh noooooo!" Tyler sounded demented with fear. He was on his hands and knees trying to scramble up the side of the crater, creating an avalanche of rocks and pebbles.

"Kat-ie!" shrieked Nicola. She was the only one close enough to have a hope of throwing a grenade.

Katie had already adjusted her grenade. Now she lifted it high above her head as if she were shooting a basketball. Nicola's breath came out in half sobs, half gasps. *Please don't drop it, please don't drop it, please don't drop it.*

The grenade shot cleanly and sharply across the air and landed right in the middle of the three Arth-Creatures, freezing them instantly.

"Oh, *fantastic* aim, Katie!" Nicola felt so weak with

relief she nearly dropped her own grenade. She took a firm grip and looked around her. Frozen Arth-Creatures were dotted across the landscape like stuffed prehistoric animals in a museum. She thought she could only count about three unfrozen Arth-Creatures left, although it was difficult to be sure, because they were standing still, too. Only their umbrella-shaped heads were sweeping back and forth as they took stock of the situation.

Sean was using the cover of the frozen Arth-Creatures to slosh his way stealthily through the mud away from the center of the crater. Tyler was climbing unsteadily to his feet, while Katie had slumped over, her elbows resting on her knees, her hands covering her face. Shimlara was running back toward them around the rim of the crater. Greta, of course, wasn't moving. She looked like a shop mannequin.

But Petronella was nowhere in sight. Nicola hadn't seen her since they disembarked from the spaceship. Was the princess fleeing? Where would she go?

Three creatures. Two grenades. Nicola had one. The princess, who Nicola couldn't find or trust, had the other. They had less than ten minutes before the frozen Arth-Creatures would start to thaw. If they weren't safely in the spaceship by then, none of them would make it off this terrible planet alive.

Nicola watched the remaining creatures carefully, her

mind racing. Should they all make a run for the spaceship now? How would they carry Greta? Should she try to throw her grenade and get them all? The distance between them was about the width of Nicola's school yard. She'd never be able to throw it that far.

I don't know what to do, she thought. For a moment her mind seemed to shut down completely. Then she had a realization. *I need to get all the unarmed people together in one spot.*

"Everyone run to Greta!" yelled Nicola. "Now!"

Nicola and Tyler got to Greta first. Nicola touched Greta's shoulder and found it was ice cold. She looked over to Sean. He was making good progress, sort of vaulting through the mud, as if he were leaping over hurdles, but then he slipped and fell. Shimlara ran out and dragged him to his feet with her good arm, and they stumbled together to join Greta, Nicola, and Tyler.

None of the Arth-Creatures seemed to be following them. Had they given up?

"Nicola!" yelled Tyler, pointing over her shoulder. Nicola swung around and saw an Arth-Creature looming directly over Katie. With a casual swipe of its paw, it knocked her to the ground, lowered its head, and opened its mouth wide.

There was no time even to think, *I'd better throw it and*

I'd better not miss. Nicola flung her arm back, aimed, and threw the grenade.

It exploded directly in front of Katie.

The Arth-Creature froze with its mouth stretched wide around Katie's head. Its vicious teeth were only millimeters away from crunching into her skull.

The purple smoke cleared. Katie carefully maneuvered her head out of the Arth-Creature's mouth, stood up, and ran toward them.

"You . . . it . . . I . . ." Katie, her eyes huge and panic-stricken, couldn't get the words out.

Nicola couldn't speak, either. She felt her knees almost give way. If she'd thrown the freeze-grenade a second later, Katie would be dead.

"How many left? How many left?" Shimlara was in a frenzy.

"Two," said Sean tersely. He pointed to the left of the crater at a particularly huge, hairy, and hungry-looking creature. "One over there."

"And another one over there." Tyler pointed to his right. It was a smaller one with intelligent eyes, looking at them shrewdly.

The Space Brigade huddled together around the immobile, unblinking Greta. They were muddy, exhausted, and terrified.

The two Arth-Creatures seemed to be communicating with each other.

"GWOOOOOARRRGGH!" roared the smaller one. *"GWOG HOGALOG MOGALOG!"*

The hairy one listened carefully. *"HWWAAA!"* it answered.

Sean was feverishly biting his nails—something Nicola had never seen him do in his entire life. "I think we're in trouble," he said.

29

**HOULD WE MAKE A RUN FOR THE SPACESHIP?"**
Sean asked Nicola.

Nicola wanted to scream, *I don't know! How should I know? You're older than me!*

Instead, she was amazed at how calm and controlled her voice sounded as she said, "We can't leave Greta. Where is the princess? She's got the last grenade."

"There she is," said Shimlara. "What's she doing?"

The princess must have run around to the other side of the crater. Now she was standing halfway between the two Arth-Creatures, with her feet firmly planted in the mud. She looked like a cowboy waiting for a duel, except of course for her mud-splattered yellow pajamas and the tiara still fixed firmly to her head.

"They're at least fifty meters apart," said Tyler. "There's no way she can get both of them with one grenade."

"Yeah, and I think the Arth-Creatures might have worked that out," said Shimlara.

The two Arth-Creatures were now wearing a smug, satisfied look, as if they were heading off to an all-you-can-eat buffet dinner.

The princess wound her arms around in circles and twisted her neck back and forth.

"She's stretching." Sean shook his head. "She's getting ready to freeze one of them. She's crazy!"

"Princess Petronella, that's our last freeze-grenade!" yelled Nicola. "We can't afford to waste it! And have you changed the setting?"

The princess just rolled her eyes.

"Maybe she wants us to die," said Shimlara.

"We did kidnap her," said Katie.

The princess turned toward the larger, hairier Arth-Creature and pointed one finger at it like a dart player taking aim.

Nicola clenched her fists tight in frustration. If the princess used up the last grenade, there would still be one creature left—the intelligent-looking one that was now rubbing its large tummy as if to say, "Good. More food for me."

"Wait till they're together so you can get both of them at once!" shouted Nicola. The princess took no notice.

Should I sacrifice myself to that last Arth-Creature so the others can escape? Nicola felt dizzy with terror as she imagined sharp, cruel teeth savaging her skin, crunching on her bones. *It will hurt immensely, but it's the right thing to do. The noble thing to do.*

The princess threw her grenade. It spun so fast it was a blur in the yellow sky.

I'll die a heroic death. Nicola's legs trembled uncontrollably. *They'll probably make a movie about me.*

The grenade hit the huge hairy Arth-Creature right in the center of the forehead with a loud *thwock* sound like a cricket ball against a bat.

But what about saving Earth? There might not be any Earthlings left to WATCH movies.

The Arth-Creature toppled backward and landed with an enormous *SPLAT* of mud. The grenade had bounced cleanly off his forehead without exploding.

Nicola's jaw dropped. *What the . . . ?*

Like spectators at a tennis match, everyone in the Space Brigade except for Greta turned their heads to watch the grenade soaring in the opposite direction across the sky. It plopped to the ground and rolled neatly to a stop, like a perfectly placed golf ball, directly in front of the intelligent Arth-Creature.

The grenade exploded.

The intelligent Arth-Creature seemed about to run, and then shrugged in resignation, as if to say, *You got me.* It froze, shoulders lifted mid-shrug, an almost admiring expression on its face.

There were a few seconds of amazed silence.

I'm not going to be eaten, thought Nicola. She felt so giddy with relief, her legs almost gave way. *I'm NOT going to be eaten! No heroic death—yippee!*

Simultaneously, Nicola, Shimlara, Sean, Tyler, and Katie erupted into cheers. Together, they sloshed through the mud toward the princess, leaving Greta behind.

They leaped around her, everyone talking at once.

"Thank you," said Nicola over and over. "Thank you, thank you, thank you!"

Tyler grabbed the princess's hand and shook it briskly, while Katie hugged her around the waist. Shimlara held up one palm and gave her a high five.

"You know what? You're one of the most annoying girls I've ever met," said Sean. "But I have to say, that was one of the coolest moves I've ever seen."

"Thanks for the compliment, *kidnapper*," answered the princess, but Nicola noticed that her cheeks were pink with pleasure.

"How did you learn to do that?" asked Katie. "You must have thrown it just right, so it didn't explode when it hit the first one."

"It's a little technique I taught myself just for the fun of it," answered the princess. "I practice on my guards. Anyway, I'd just love to sit around and have a picnic with you all, but that big unconscious Arth-Creature could wake up at any moment, and the rest of the Arth-Creatures will be unfreezing soon. Don't you think you should maybe get on with the job of kidnapping me?"

"Ah, yep, sure," said Nicola. She felt awkward now that the princess had helped save the day.

"Want to tie me up again?" asked the princess. "Tape my mouth?"

"Um, no, that's okay."

"So, I guess we really shouldn't leave Greta behind?" said Sean, surveying her frozen figure.

"We'll have to carry her on to the spaceship somehow," said Nicola.

Shimlara said to the princess, "Come on, Your Royal muddy Highness, you can help Sean and me carry Greta. We're so much taller than these Earthling squirts!"

"Great," said the princess. "Not only do I have to save my kidnappers' lives, now I have to help lug you around!" But she went off willingly with Shimlara and grabbed hold of Greta under her frozen arms. Sean took one of Greta's legs, and Shimlara took the other with her unbroken arm. Together they hauled Greta over toward the spaceship as though she were a piece of furniture.

"I feel *bad* about kidnapping the princess now," said Katie quietly as they trudged toward the spaceship.

"I know what you mean," said Nicola.

"Don't forget the princess plans to destroy our planet," Tyler pointed out.

"Actually, I think she's sort of having fun," said Katie.

Nicola looked over at the princess as she helped Sean and Shimlara shove Greta headfirst into the spaceship. "You might be right. Do you think that means she might change her mind about the garbage can?"

"Does Mrs. Zucchini ever change her mind about giving a math test?" Tyler asked.

"No."

"Exactly."

30

IT WAS DIFFICULT FIGURING OUT WHAT TO DO WITH Greta. She was frozen so solid, it was impossible to bend her in half to sit her in one of the seats. In the end, Sean suggested strapping her down in the section for baggage at the back of the spaceship.

"I'd say we've only got about two minutes before she starts to thaw," said Shimlara. "She's going to be in a bad mood."

"Yeah, she'll blame you, Nicola," said Tyler as he very carefully typed the letters "B-U-D-D-Y B-E-A-C-H, A-U-S-T-R-A-L-I-A, E-A-R-T-H," while Katie looked over his shoulder to double-check there were no mistakes this time.

"Speaking of unfreezing . . ." The princess pointed with her chin out the window. The first Arth-Creatures they'd frozen were starting to twitch and the big one the princess had knocked out was sitting up and shaking its huge head. "You'd better hurry up."

"Esteemedpassengerspreparefortakeoff!" garbled Tyler. He slammed the red button and once again they hurtled across a star-spangled sky, leaving the Arth-Creatures a million light years behind them.

"Ah, spaceship travel." Sean stuck his feet out and tipped his head back comfortably against the seats. "This is starting to seem as normal as catching the school bus."

"No chewing gum under the seats," said Katie.

"I can soon fix that," said Sean.

I hope we get the right planet this time, thought Nicola as she closed her eyes, just for a second. *I'm too tired to battle any more creatures.*

"WHAT IS GOING ON HERE?! WHY CAN'T I MOVE? WHY AM I LYING ON THE FLOOR? *WHY AM I ALL WET . . . AND MUDDY . . . AND ITCHY, ITCHY, ITCHY!*"

Nicola's eyes flew open. What a pity, Greta's mouth was starting to thaw before the rest of her.

"NICOLA BERRY! This is all your fault!"

"Told you," said Tyler quietly.

"Actually, Greta," said Shimlara. "It's all *your* fault for dropping the freeze-grenade. I think you have a word on your planet, is it Butterfingers? Well, Butterfingers, it's just lucky that Katie stepped in and saved the day, otherwise some Arth-Creature would be eating Tyler on Toast right now."

Sean snorted.

"I'M ITCHY!" moaned Greta.

"Don't worry, Greta," said Nicola. "I'm getting Tyler to take us to Buddy Beach, so we can all have a swim and wash off the mud."

"Pfff! Tyler will probably land us on a snowfield on Mars!"

"Well, Earthling, I'm sure he'll do a better job flying the spaceship than you did throwing that freeze-grenade," said Princess Petronella. "Your mistake nearly cost your friend his life."

Tyler and Nicola exchanged surprised glances at this unexpected show of support. Greta seemed to be struck dumb.

Tyler cleared his throat. "Right! Well, esteemed passengers, please fasten your seat belts for landing. I'm pretty sure this time we're heading down toward Earth. If you look to your left, you'll see our beautiful planet just beneath us."

Nicola craned her head and caught her breath.

There was Earth—silent and majestic, round as a marble, floating in space like an exquisite Christmas tree decoration. *That's my planet*, thought Nicola, and she was filled with a strange, teary, proud feeling. It was interesting how she'd felt proud of her family before (when they weren't embarrassing her) and proud of her friends. She'd felt proud of her soccer team when it scored a goal and proud of her country when it won Olympic medals—but she'd never ever thought to feel proud of her planet. Katie spoke up, and Nicola was surprised at how strong and confident her friend sounded. "Princess Petronella," she said. "See those patches of blue? Those are oceans. That's what we'll be swimming in."

"That's an ocean?" said the princess. "It's not like I imagined!"

"Wait till you see an ocean up close," said Nicola. She tried to think of the right words to describe it. "It's so huge and beautiful, and when the sun shines on the water, it's like a carpet of glittering diamonds stretching out as far as you can see."

"Really?" The princess sounded excited and bubbly, like a normal girl on vacation.

"YIKES!" Suddenly Tyler swerved the spaceship to one side as a tiny silver pellet streaked toward them like a bullet. "We only just missed it!"

"What was it?" asked Nicola.

"I think it was space junk!" Tyler looked delighted. "It's all this stuff left over from old space missions, like nuts, bolts, and old satellites from fifty years ago! It might even have been an astronaut's old glove! I've read there are over *one hundred thousand* pieces of space junk. It's like a huge orbiting piece of garb—oh." Tyler bit his lip and stopped talking. He obviously didn't want to say the word "garbage" in front of the princess and remind her of her plans for Earth. There was silence on the spaceship as everybody tried to think of a new, safer topic of conversation.

The princess spoke again and this time she didn't sound bubbly at all. "Don't think I've forgotten that this is a KID-NAPPING. I've been reading all your minds, and I know you think once I see your pathetic little excuse of a planet, I'll have a change of heart about using it for an intergalactic garbage can. But you might be interested to know, I have never changed my mind about anything in my whole life. Never have, never will."

ITH A FEW DEFT TWISTS OF THE CONTROLS
and a slight frown between his eyes, Tyler
landed the spaceship as gently as a bird
gliding to the ground.

"I think you're just as good a pilot as
Plum now!" said Shimlara.

"Let's see which planet we're on first," said Tyler modestly.

Sean unbuckled his seat belt and leaped to his feet. He pulled the lever on the door.

"Welcome to the planet of . . . ORTH!"

"Ha, ha, very funny." Nicola shoved him aside so she could see out.

Golden sunlight flooded the spaceship. This time, the smell that filled her nostrils was something delicious and familiar. It was a mixture of salty ocean, French fries, and sunscreen. It was the smell of the beach.

"Check it out, Nic." Sean pointed at a familiar old battered wooden sign in the distance. It had a picture of a smiling lobster with a speech bubble saying:

WELCOME TO BUDDY BEACH!

The Berry family had spent every vacation at Buddy Beach since Sean and Nicola were very little. They slept in a trailer that they kept permanently on a grassy patch of land right at the end of the beach. Nicola had always said it was her favorite place in the world. Now, after the horror of Arth, she thought it might be her favorite place in the galaxy.

"What's the plan?" Sean asked Nicola quietly.

"I don't know." Nicola brushed some dried Arth mud from her face and lowered her voice so the others couldn't hear. "I just thought we could give the princess a typical Earth experience. Take her swimming, toast marshmallows for her, that sort of thing. Then I'll ask her one more time. I don't know what else to do. Mully said I needed to become friends with the princess, but I don't know if that's possible."

"You're doing a great job, Nic," said Sean.

"Um . . . thank you." Wow. Even if they didn't save the world, one good thing to come out of this was that her big brother actually seemed to *respect* her now.

"Oh no, look over there!" Sean grabbed Nicola's shoulder. "It's the guards from the palace and a pack of Arth-Creatures!"

"What?"

Nicola spun in the direction he was pointing, banging her elbow against the side of the spaceship.

Sean fell about laughing. "Ha! Made you look, made you look!"

Hmmm. Maybe not much had changed after all.

"Come on, everybody," she said. "Let's go have a swim and wash off this mud."

Everybody unbuckled their seat belts and stood up.

"Actually," said Nicola carefully. "I think the princess should go first."

"Hmmmph," sniffed the princess. She tucked a curl of limp, muddy hair behind her ear, straightened her dirty tiara, and even though she was wearing muddy pj's she walked regally to the door as if she were at a ball.

This is it, thought Nicola. *This is our last chance to save the planet.*

She stood back and gestured toward the open door.

"Princess Petronella . . ." She spoke in a loud, formal voice. "Welcome to our planet. Welcome to Earth."

HE SUN WAS WARM ON THEIR CLAMMY, MUDDY
skin. They could hear waves gently thumping on
the sand and the shrieks of seagulls. The sea was a
giant glittery curve stretching out to the horizon.
It was *perfect*. Nobody could resist Buddy Beach.

The princess walked slowly down the stairs of the
spaceship and onto the rippled gold sand.

"I bet she loves it!" whispered Katie behind Nicola.
"This was such a good—"

"AAAAAAAUUUGGH!"

The princess jumped madly from foot to foot. "Hot,
burning, hot, hot, hot! What is this horrible yellow dirt?"

Oh great, the sand was boiling hot, and of course, the
princess was the only one of them with bare feet. Couldn't
things go right for just a second?

"Stand on this!" Greta, who was still half frozen but
had thawed enough to walk, stiffly pulled a raincoat from
her schoolbag and threw it down onto the sand in front of
the princess, who jumped on it, her face screwed up in pain.

"That *hurt*! Did you do that on purpose? After I saved
all your pathetic little lives? I'm going to get the palace

torturers to add special foot-torture to your treatments!"

This was not going well at all.

"We didn't do it on purpose," said Nicola as the rest of the Space Brigade joined her on the beach. "I'm sorry. I just forgot the sand would be hot. See, it happens to everybody!"

She pointed to a surfer in the distance who was dashing along the beach on his tiptoes.

"Well, even if you didn't do it on purpose, what sort of planet has a ground so hot you can't walk on it?"

"It's only the sand," said Nicola. "Grass is fine to walk on."

"Unless there are burrs," said Greta.

"What are burrs?" asked the princess.

"They're sharp things that stick in your feet. Like glass."

"Thanks very much, Greta," said Nicola.

"I'm just being truthful. Gosh, I'm so *itchy*!"

A little boy's voice piped up in the distance.

"Mommy, Mommy, I just saw a spaceship land on the beach over there! Come and see!"

A woman's voice answered, "Very imaginative, darling."

"No, no, I *saw* it!"

"Oh dear," said Nicola. "I don't want us attracting huge crowds of people."

"That's okay," said Shimlara. "The mini spaceships are great because they're portable. Look."

She went to the side of the spaceship and pressed a row of buttons. The spaceship began whirling slowly around in circles. It spun faster and faster until it was just a blur of color, like a cake mixer on full blast. Then suddenly it stopped and seemed to disappear completely. Sitting on the sand was an unassuming silver briefcase with the words MINI EASY-RIDE SPACESHIP written discreetly on the side. Shimlara picked up the briefcase in one hand. "See?"

"Fabulous!" said Tyler.

"Yes, fabulous, a run-of-the-mill cheap-brand mini spaceship," said the princess. "So am I stuck on this raincoat forever?"

"You can borrow my shoes," offered Shimlara. "I think we're about the same size."

"I won't be borrowing them. I'll be confiscating them! Hand them over, now!"

Shimlara snapped, "Not if you ask like that! May I remind you that *we're* the kidnappers and *you're* the hostage, and by the way, that mini spaceship was a present from my mom and dad!"

"Who are no doubt being captured by my guards right now!" said the princess.

There was silence for a moment and everybody looked at Nicola expectantly.

Sometimes, when Nicola's dad was trying to cook dinner and everything was burning and he kept running out of ingredients, he said that he felt like his head was going to explode. For the first time, Nicola understood exactly what he meant.

"Ummmm," she began. "Ahhh."

She really had no idea what to do or say next. It was all getting to be too much. What she really wanted to say was, "Can I have a break from being the boss now?"

Luckily, everybody began to speak at once.

"Well, I'll run over to the trailer and get some spare flip-flops for the princess," said Sean.

"I'll come with you and collect swimsuits and towels for everybody," said Katie.

"I'll get boogie boards," said Tyler. "The surf looks great!"

"I'll come and help you," said Shimlara. "I've never seen a trailer, or a boogie board. Can you fly them?"

"Well, I'm just going to sit here and *thaw* and *itch*." Greta plonked herself down on the sand in a puddle of water.

The princess sat down on Greta's raincoat and rubbed her feet. "I'm going to enjoy planning individual torture treatments for each of you."

"Take your time," said Nicola.

For the first time in ages, she looked at her countdown watch.

HOORAY! THIS IS IT! YOUR LAST DAY
BEFORE THE DREADED DEADLINE!
NOW IS THE TIME FOR ANY LAST
MINUTE FINISHING TOUCHES!

Finishing touches! She was trying to save the world, not prepare for a dinner party!

"You've got no idea how hard this is," she hissed at her watch.

"Talking to yourself, are you?" sneered the princess. "That's the first sign of insanity."

Nicola sighed. Making friends with this girl was going to be about as easy as making friends with Mrs. Zucchini.

33

TWENTY MINUTES LATER, EVERYONE WAS STANDING on the hard, cool sand at the edge of the surf.

Luckily there were plenty of spare old bathing suits in the Berry family trailer, and Greta had packed her Honeyville Primary swim-team uniform in her schoolbag. Shimlara and the princess were wearing suits belonging to Nicola's mom because they were both about her height. Katie had helped Shimlara wrap a plastic bag around her cast, using a rubber band to hold it in place.

Nicola kept sneaking looks up at the princess. It was funny, Nicola's mom's simple, one-piece bathing suit made the princess look like such a *normal* girl. Well, nearly a normal girl—except that she was extraordinarily tall and she still insisted on wearing her tiara, even though they had all told her it would surely fall off in the surf.

The princess had white, freckly skin, and Nicola said that she had to wear sunscreen or she'd get badly sunburned and that would hurt even more than the hot sand.

"So you only have one sun on this planet, and the one you have *burns your skin*?" the princess said with disbelief, while Nicola briskly rubbed sunscreen onto her back.

Now the princess shaded her eyes as she looked out at the ocean. "Why does the water move up and down like that?"

"It's the wind," explained Tyler. "They're called waves."

"So, how do you swim around them?" Shimlara looked worried. "Don't they get in your way?"

"I would think they must be very annoying," said the princess imperiously.

"Nah, they're great! You just dive under them," said Sean. "I'll show you."

He ran straight into the water and dived under a wave. He came up with his hair plastered flat against his head, grinned, and dived under another one.

"Oh, no, I can't do that." Shimlara held her palms up and started backing away from the water.

"You don't have to dive under them," said Katie. "You can jump over them, or you can kick your legs and float gently over the top of them."

"Or if they're too big to jump over, you can hold your nose and duck," said Tyler.

"Come on, Tyler and Greta, let's do a demonstration," said Katie.

"Yes, well, I was just *about* to suggest that myself," said Greta.

They ran into the water. Greta ducked under a wave pointing at her head, while Katie floated over it with her arms up like a ballerina, and Tyler jumped through the middle of it.

"The way the nice Earthling did it looks quite easy," said the princess thoughtfully.

Aha, thought Nicola, *so the princess thinks Katie is nice—that's something.*

"Oooh!" Shimlara squealed and gurgled as a bigger wave splashed up past her knees. *It is like taking little kids to the beach,* thought Nicola. *Just really, really tall little kids.*

"Let's all go in together," she said.

"Okay!" Shimlara grabbed Nicola's hand and, after a second's hesitation, the princess grabbed the other one.

Together they walked into the ocean. As the water frothed around her waist, Nicola tried to imagine what it must be like for Shimlara and the princess. It was probably like the first time she went cloud-swimming: an entirely new experience that had been both incredibly exciting and incredibly scary.

Luckily, the first wave was a small, gentle one. Shimlara and the princess both obediently held up their arms like ballerinas, exactly as Katie had done, and Nicola tried to keep a straight face.

"That was fun!" Shimlara trod water, a huge smile on her face.

"I suppose it's an interesting sensation," said the princess coolly as they floated over another one. "Oooh, this one looks *big*!" She clutched Nicola's arm, nearly pushing her under.

An unexpectedly huge wave was coming their way. Before it reached them, it curled over and broke into a frenzy of white water. There was no way they could float or even jump over it.

"You're going to have to duck under it!" shouted Tyler.

If the princess gets dumped, thought Nicola, *it will be the last straw*. The mission would be lost.

"Take a breath! Curl up like a ball!" she yelled. "You'll be—"

There was no time to say "okay." Just before she ducked, she caught a glimpse of Shimlara and the princess both holding their noses tightly, their eyes big with fear.

Nicola ducked down as low as she could. The water grabbed hold of her and shook her back and forth and around and around like a shirt in a washing machine. She opened her eyes and all she could see was white, swirling water. Which way was up? What was happening to the princess and Shimlara?

She popped back up and the water was calm and

sparkling. She looked around frantically. Where were they?

"WHOA!" Shimlara's head broke through the water and she gasped for air. "I ducked straight under that *gigantic* wall of water! Did you see me, Nicola?"

"Umm—well—"

"WHOA!" It was the princess, her wet hair plastered over her face like seaweed, but her tiara, amazingly, still on her head. She pushed her hair out of her eyes impatiently. "I did it! Did you see me? Did you see what I did?"

"I saw you both! You were *fantastic*!" Katie swam up to them. "You did it perfectly!" The princess and Shimlara beamed and Nicola understood that they both had wanted to be praised. It must have been Katie's experience with her little brothers that helped her know the right thing to say.

"You were both great!" she agreed.

"Yep, I think you're ready to try *catching* a wave now." Sean and Tyler appeared next to them, paddling on the boogie boards they'd picked up from the trailer.

"Catch one?" said Shimlara. "How could we catch one? And what would we do with it when we caught it?"

"I don't think they're ready to try boogie boarding yet," said Nicola, giving Sean a warning look. No need to rush things.

"Why? Is boogie boarding just for boys?" asked Shimlara.

"No!" cried Nicola, Katie, and Greta all at the same time, in the same horrified tone of voice.

"Then I shall try it," said the princess. "I was very good at wave-ducking. I expect I will be outstanding at boogie boarding. Demonstrate it to me, Earthling Boy."

"Actually, you can call me Sean, Alien Girl," said Sean.

"Oh!" Nicola spoke quickly, hoping that the princess hadn't heard the Alien Girl part over the crashing of the waves. "You don't even know our names! We were so busy kidnapping you, we forgot to introduce ourselves. How rude!"

"I'm Katie," shouted Katie as they all jumped over a wave. "I'd curtsy, but it's a bit hard while we're swimming."

"You may kiss my hand instead." The princess graciously held out her hand.

"Come off it!" exploded Sean. "I'm not kissing any girl's hand, even if you are a princess. I'm Sean, that's Tyler, Greta, Shimlara, Katie, and Nic-the-boss. We're pleased to meet you and we're pleased to kidnap you. Now do you want to try boogie boarding or not?"

Nicola was going to *murder* Sean. She hoped he suffocated under a huge pile of garbage, because if this mission failed it would be his fault.

The princess narrowed her eyes dangerously. "Yes, I do want to try it, *Sean*."

"Good! Tyler can show you what to do. On you go." Sean slid off the board and helped the princess lie down on the board and adjust the ankle strap.

"Nicola, you should put a stop to this," hissed Greta. "She'll fall off and she'll be mad and the mission will fail."

"Do you think?" said Nicola vaguely, but she knew there was nothing she could do to stop them. It didn't matter how much she yelled at them, the princess and Sean were both too stubborn to listen.

Tyler showed the princess how to paddle with her hands and kick with her legs. "You're not wearing flippers, so you'll have to kick really hard."

"You!" The princess pointed at Greta. "Get me some of those flipper things immediately!"

Greta frowned. "On this planet we say *please*."

"We don't have any flippers in your size, Princess." Sean swung her board around so it was facing the shore. "Anyway, I'm going to give you a push, so just enjoy the ride. Whatever you do, don't look behind you!"

A beautiful, smooth, curling wave was heading toward them. It was perfect for boogie boarding but it was *very* big.

"Not that one, Sean!" called out Nicola. "At least try a smaller one."

Sean cupped his hand behind his ear and frowned, shrugging his shoulders and pretending that he couldn't hear what she was saying. Oh, for goodness sake.

"Ooh, I don't want to watch!" Katie covered her eyes.

"Is he trying to kill her?" asked Shimlara with interest.

The wave was nearly upon them. The princess paddled her hands and kicked her legs, imitating Tyler. She looked very determined. Nicola had to admire her.

"Now hold on tight!" Sean gave the boogie board an almighty shove.

Clinging on to the sides of the board, the princess plunged headfirst over the crest of the wave. "WHOOOEEEEEEE!" she shrieked as her tiara flew straight off her head and the board streaked toward the shore.

"She's going too fast," said Greta. "She's going to—"

The boogie board flipped over and the princess flew through the air, her arms and legs flailing before she crashed into the water.

"Ouch," winced Shimlara.

"Uh-oh," said Katie.

They watched Tyler paddling his board over to the princess.

"You've made a lot of mistakes, but I'd say that was your worst yet, Nicola," remarked Greta in a satisfied way.

"I'm sorry, Nic," said Sean glumly.

Suddenly the princess erupted out of the water. She caught sight of Tyler and lunged toward him, dragging her boogie board behind her, yelling something they couldn't understand.

"Quick! She's going to kill him," said Nicola. She started to swim over to them, but Sean grabbed her arm, holding her back. He was smiling. What was there to smile about? This was no time for jokes!

"Listen," he said.

Nicola listened.

The princess was shouting, *"Again! Again! I want to do it again!"*

T WAS MUCH LATER THAT DAY, AND THE SPACE
Brigade and Princess Petronella sat on the beach
wearing old sweats from the trailer. Greta had surprised them by efficiently finding firewood and
building a perfect campfire the way she'd learned to
in Girl Scouts.

After swimming, they'd all gone food shopping at the
local supermarket (where a girl had approached the princess and Shimlara and *begged* them to consider joining her
basketball team).

Now Tyler was showing Shimlara how to fry sausages,
while Sean toasted bread rolls on the fire, and Katie and
Nicola chopped tomatoes. Greta was making disapproving
remarks about their cooking techniques and everybody
was ignoring her.

"So every single time you want something to eat you
have to *cook* it yourself?" The princess was stunned that
they didn't have Telepathy Chefs on Earth yet.

"Cooking is fun," Tyler told the princess. "You can help
us by buttering the rolls if you like."

"I am not trained in the art of 'buttering a roll,' Tyler,"

said the princess. Her hair had fallen out of its bun and was curling in messy tendrils all around her shoulders. She actually looked rather pretty in the crackling light of the fire.

"You just dip the knife in the butter, like so," said Sean, demonstrating. "And then smear across the toast. Not too thick. Not too thin. It's not exactly an art."

To everyone's surprise, the princess took the knife from him and tentatively began buttering the rolls.

"Oh, look, the colors of the sky are changing!" Shimlara pointed at the horizon, where the sky was turning pink and gold. She explained, "The suns on Globagaskar don't go down slowly like that each night. They just disappear at six o'clock, as if someone has switched off a light."

Nicola said, "Every time there's an extra-beautiful sunset, our mom makes us run outside to watch."

"Yeah, she won't even let us wait for the commercial break," complained Sean.

"It's *really* beautiful," said the princess quietly, almost as if she were speaking to herself.

"Go, Earth!" whispered Shimlara, while Sean did a silent victory punch in the air behind the princess's back.

Something is probably about to go wrong again, thought Nicola. But her luck must have been changing, because at that moment she felt a delicate flutter against the top of her hand. It was a butterfly. Its wings were black with an intricate pattern of blue spots like wrapping paper.

"Oh look, a butterfly," said Nicola casually. "Do you have butterflies on Globagaskar, Princess Petronella?" Of course, she knew perfectly well that they didn't. She held out her wrist to the princess.

"No, we don't have flying butters." The princess looked enchanted as the butterfly flew straight onto her hand, almost as if it knew it had to help out with the mission. It flew up near the princess's face and caressed her cheek with its wings before it flew off. That butterfly deserved a medal.

"You just got a butterfly kiss," said Katie. "Now you'll have good luck."

"Really?" The princess seemed quite dazed.

"Okay!" said Tyler briskly. "I think the sausages are nearly ready. How are those rolls going?"

The princess bent her head obediently. "Nearly done."

As Nicola looked around, she saw that every member of the Space Brigade, even Greta, was trying to suppress a giant grin. Things were looking up.

She sneaked a look at her countdown watch. It said:

TOMORROW IS THE DAY—ARE YOU NEARLY DONE?
IF NOT . . . PANIC NOW!!!

For once, Nicola didn't feel like throwing the watch on the ground and smashing it into a million pieces. There was actually no need to panic. Things were progressing well. After they'd eaten dinner, she would very politely but firmly ask the princess if she would please change her mind about destroying Earth.

The princess would say "sure, no problem" and apologize profusely for even considering such a thing. After that they would all go to sleep on the beach in their sleeping bags, and the next morning after a delicious celebratory breakfast, they would fly the princess back to Globagaskar.

Then Nicola could relax and enjoy her birthday. She would probably receive particularly excellent presents because everybody would be so pleased with her.

Of course, on the other hand, the palace guards could be about to track them down on Earth any second now, the princess could refuse to change her mind (after all, she'd never changed her mind about anything before), and Nicola and the rest of the Space Brigade could be spending her birthday being tortured while Earth was being destroyed.

Tomorrow was either going to be Nicola's very best birthday ever—or her very worst.

**SK NOW! HURRY UP AND ASK HER!**

Nicola wasn't saying a word out loud, but inside her head she was yelling and screaming at herself like Mrs. Zucchini on the hottest day of the year.

They'd eaten the sausages and Princess Petronella had called them "strangely delicious." She had also gotten a bad attack of the hiccups after drinking a can of Coke and had actually *giggled* when Sean had teased her about it. Then she'd said the stars in the sky reminded her of the diamonds on the Rainbow Palace back home and had commented on the fact that even though the "yellow dirt" had burned her earlier, it had quite an "unusual texture." Now they were all toasting marshmallows on sticks in the fire, and the princess was asking lots of interested, polite questions.

She hadn't said one nasty thing about Earth, or in fact one nasty thing at all, for ages. Nicola was almost starting to *like* her, for heaven's sakes! Now was the absolutely perfect time to ask, but she was suffering from a terrible attack of nerves. She couldn't bear to see the princess turn back into her bossy, hard, princessy self, and if she said no, what then? Nicola was all out of ideas.

She shouted silently at herself: *STOP BEING SUCH A COWARDLY CUSTARD!*

It's okay, Nicola, just relax and take your time. You've done a great job so far.

It was Shimlara's voice inside her head. Nicola looked around for her and saw that she was lying on her stomach on the opposite side of the fire, not even looking at Nicola.

Nicola responded, *I thought it was bad manners to read people's minds without their permission!*

Ooops! Sorry! It's just that you were yelling so loud in your head, I couldn't help but overhear it!

The princess held up her stick and said, "Can I eat my mershmullow yet?"

"Marshmallow," corrected Katie gently. She examined the princess's marshmallow. "A perfect golden color! Go ahead."

The princess opened her mouth to swallow it whole and everybody yelled out at the same time, "CAREFUL, IT'S *HOT*!"

The princess stopped with her mouth still open and stared at them.

"Thank you." She smiled, and nibbled at the side of the

marshmallow. "Mmmm, yum! It's all soft and sticky on the inside!"

"Whenever we go camping," commented Sean, "Mom always burns her marshmallows black. Every single time. She starts talking and forgets what she's doing."

Nicola laughed. "Yes, and she gets so angry and surprised each time it happens!"

"Do you get to go on vacations with your parents?" asked the princess.

"Of course," said Sean. "Don't you?"

"Never," said the princess. "They like to go on big trekking vacations to mountainous planets and they say my legs are too short to keep up. Plus, someone has to stay at the palace and be in charge of things."

Greta said, "My parents never take me on vacations, either. They're always going away for big work conferences and they say I'd be bored. So I have to go on vacations with my Auntie Bev, and all she does is *knit* and *drink cups of tea*! It makes me so *angry*!"

"I know! Me too!" said the princess with surprise.

"Sometimes," said Greta, "I'm in such a bad mood, I'm really mean to my Auntie Bev, and I make her cry. Then I feel guilty because it's not her fault."

"I *know*!" The princess looked really excited. "I make all my servants cry, too! I make them scrub floors even when they don't need scrubbing! Is that what you do to your Auntie Bev?"

"Ah, not exactly," admitted Greta.

"And when I'm feeling really cranky," continued the princess, "I do even BIGGER things, like I might just order the army to go and destroy some random planet—oh."

The princess stopped talking and suddenly seemed to remember where she was. Was she actually *blushing*? There was silence, except for the crackling of the fire and the crash of waves.

Interesting. Nicola thought about how sad and difficult it must be to have parents who don't even like you enough to go on vacations with you. She remembered how she'd convinced her mom and dad to take her and Sean to the mountains in New Zealand last winter and what a fantastic time they'd all had, even though Nicola's mom really hadn't wanted to go in the first place. She'd thought it would be too cold. Nicola had spent ages convincing her to change her mind, describing all the parts she knew would appeal to her mom—like hot chocolate by the fire and beautiful ski slopes and Sean and Nicola not fighting at all (which had *nearly* turned out to be true).

Actually . . . that was an example of a time Nicola *had* convinced someone to change their mind when their mind was already made up!

So Georgio hadn't needed to change that last question after all. Her answer to that question should have been *yes*. She could do it! She *was* the right person for the job. It was all a matter of understanding the other person's point of view and caring about them enough to try to understand what mattered to them.

Nicola decided it was now or never.

She said, "Have you had a good time today, Princess Petronella?"

The princess lifted her chin. She said, "I think I've had the best day of my whole life."

YES! Nicola did cartwheels inside her head.

She stood up on the sand. She felt a bit stupid, but it seemed the right thing to do.

"Princess Petronella, as the Earthling Ambassador, I would first like to apologize for kidnapping you. We didn't know what else to do. We just wanted you to see our planet for yourself. As you can see, although it's not perfect, it's beautiful, and it's our home, and we love it."

She took a breath. Tyler nodded at her encouragingly.

"I'd also like to thank you again for your help on Arth. We wouldn't have survived if it wasn't for you. So, I know I've already asked you this question once before, but I'm going to ask it again. Princess Petronella, will you please change your mind about turning Earth into a garbage can? *Please?*"

The princess stood up, too.

She said, "Okay, I must admit, I *was* planning to cut off all of your heads and place them around the palace walls as a warning to other kidnappers—ha ha!"

She stopped laughing when she saw the expressions on their faces.

"Sorry. Yes. Not that funny. Anyway, I was pretty mad at you, but then I don't know why—this has never happened to me before and it's unbelievable, considering that I'm *royalty* and you're all just ordinary people, not even *nobility,* and apart from Shimlara, you're *Earthlings*—but the thing is, I started to sort of . . . *like you.*"

"We like you, too!" said Katie generously.

"Sort of," added Sean.

"Plus," continued the princess, "I like this funny planet. It's fun capturing waves and being kissed by flying butters. That's why I've decided—"

BA-BOOM! BA-BOOM! BA-BOOM!

Suddenly, they couldn't hear a word she was saying. Everybody put their hands over their ears as a sound like a thousand firecrackers exploded above them.

They looked up.

It was like the sky had been ripped in two by giant hands and then set on fire.

Through the gap in the flaming sky, a huge spaceship, the size of a *mountain*, zoomed straight toward the beach.

Nicola gulped for air like a drowning person.

Was it the end of the world already? Was she too late?

T'S GOING TO LAND ON US! IT'S GOING TO LAND ON us!" shrieked Greta with her hands over her head, as if that would be enough to protect her from a crashing spaceship.

"It's not! It's going to land in the water," yelled Tyler, his head tipped back to look up at the blaze.

He was right.

The spaceship crashed straight into the ocean.

WHOOMPA!

It hit the water with such a splash, an enormous wave of cold water crashed on to the beach, drenching them all and putting out their fire.

For a second or two, nobody moved. They stood still, catching their breath and dripping, while their campfire hissed sadly.

"My *mershmullow*!" The princess threw down her stick with its soggy marshmallow and stamped her foot. "Why do my mom and dad have to ruin *everything*?!"

"Your mom and dad?" said Nicola. "You mean the king and queen of Globagaskar? Is that their spaceship?"

"Yes, that's the stupid Royal Spaceship." The princess stuck her lower lip out and kicked at the sand.

Nobody spoke. They all stared at the huge, glittering Royal Spaceship. It was like an entire shopping center had materialized.

"Look," said Tyler.

A long door slid open along one side of the spaceship and a metal walkway sprang out across the water to the beach.

Immediately, about fifty palace guards came jogging briskly across the walkway, each cradling a different scary-looking weapon. As they got to the beach they fell to the ground and began wriggling across the sand on their stomachs.

"Oh, for crying out loud," said the princess. She walked toward the spaceship waving her hands above her head. "MOM AND DAD! I'M OVER HERE! I'M FINE!"

A man and woman came running down the walkway, both of them clutching their jewel-encrusted crowns, purple velvet capes billowing behind them.

"Our darling NELLY!" they cried.

"Nelly?" smirked Sean.

The king and queen stumbled up the beach and threw their arms around the princess.

"Are you all right? Are you hungry? Are you warm enough? Where is your *tiara*? Oh, no, you're all WET! Did those dastardly kidnappers do that to you?"

"*YOU* got me all wet when you landed the spaceship in the water." The princess pulled away from them. "And they're not dastardly kidnappers! They're my . . . friends."

The queen gasped. "Oh, no! They've *brainwashed* you!"

"They have not!"

"But Nelly, darling." The king lifted his crown and scratched at his balding head. "We hear you gave an order to turn their planet into a garbage can. I don't think these Earthlings would really appreciate that."

"Yes, but what I was *about* to say, just before you turned up, was that—"

The princess took a breath and turned away from her father to face Nicola. "I've changed my mind," she said. "I think Earth is a funny, strange, beautiful planet, and you're very lucky it's your home. I should never have said I'd destroy it. I'm sorry."

Nicola felt such a fizzy happy feeling she thought she might float away like a balloon. YES! The mission was successful! At last!

The king and queen looked at their daughter, aghast. "Darling, we're royalty. We don't say that word!"

"What word?"

"That word beginning with *s*."

"But I *am* sorry."

"It doesn't matter. You should never admit it out loud.

Otherwise people will think we're just like them and that we can make mistakes."

"But I did make a mistake."

The queen threw up her hands in frustration. "Nelly, you're going to be the death of me!"

The king said, "Let's just not hear that sort of language again, Nelly. Now it's true that we would never have approved of your decision to destroy Earth. It's such a dear little planet! What were you thinking? Why not destroy *Arth* if you felt like destroying a planet? So, we're glad you've come to your senses about that, but there is no need to act like a commoner and apologize. We don't speak like that in our family."

"Okay, fine, whatever," said the princess. "Do you think you could just go away now? We were toasting marshmallows and then we're going to sleep on the beach and boogie on waves before breakfast!"

The king and queen looked baffled.

"Obviously we have to take your kidnappers straight off to jail," said the king. "They must be tortured!"

The Space Brigade moved closer to each other, their faces ashen.

"But they're my *friends*!" wailed the princess. "I've never had friends before!"

The queen said soothingly, "Well, we'll only torture

them the *teeniest* bit, and keep their jail sentences to twenty years! That's more than generous."

"Generous?" muttered Sean.

"But I don't want them locked away in jail. I want to keep them in my room!"

It seemed that the princess still had a bit to learn about friendship.

"Excuse me," said Greta. "We may be your friends, but we're not your *toys*."

"See, they're not even friendly!" pointed out the king. "They must go straight to jail. What sort of example would it be to the rest of the galaxy if we just let anybody kidnap us when they don't like our decisions? Guards, bring out the other prisoners—we'll handcuff them all together for convenience!"

Other prisoners?

They all looked toward the spaceship as the guards roughly pulled out two handcuffed people.

It was Shimlara who recognized them first.

"MOM and DAD! Hey! Stop pushing my parents around like that, you big bullies!"

Georgio and Mully shuffled down the walkway, both still wearing their pajamas, their ankles chained and their hands cuffed in front of them.

"Ahoy there!" cried Georgio cheerfully. "What a superb

Earth beach! Have you been swimming in an Earth ocean, Shimlara?! I'm very envious!"

"Oh dear, all of you are *drenched*!" said Mully. "You'll catch colds!"

Mully sounded just like an ordinary mom, but Nicola noticed her eyes sharply darting back and forth, looking for possible escape routes, just like a soldier.

Mully's voice popped into Nicola's head. *Don't worry, Nicola. There's always hope. Even when it seems hopeless. Oh! And my sincere apologies for so rudely talking in your head like this.*

"Right," said the king. "Handcuff them all together, please. Hurry up! We must get them tortured and jailed lickety-split, so the queen and I can get back to our vacation!"

A huge guard seized Nicola's wrist and cuffed her.

Meanwhile the princess was having a tantrum. Sand flew as she stomped her feet. "I was having FUN! For the first time ever in my WHOLE life I was having fun and now you have to RUIN it, just because they kidnapped me! Who cares if they kidnapped me?"

Suddenly Nicola had an idea. "But remember, Princess Petronella, we *didn't* actually kidnap you, did we?"

Sean caught on fast. "That's right. I was innocently dropping off a friendly invitation to a pool party when you woke up and asked if you could come to Earth with us! We said, sure, why not?!"

The princess stopped crying and stomping and looked at them carefully.

"Ah! A perfectly understandable misunderstanding, Your Most Royal Highnesses!" cried Georgio. "Kids, eh?!"

The king and queen didn't look impressed.

"Is that true, Nelly?" the king said. "Because if it is, you'll have to be punished quite severely!"

"Yes, that's right." The queen put her hands on her hips. "You can't go running off with strange Earthlings in the middle of the night whenever it suits you! If this is true, you're in very BIG trouble, young lady! You'll have to . . . you'll have to . . ."

The queen seemed to be casting about her mind for a suitable punishment. She finished triumphantly, "You'll have to make your own bed for an entire YEAR!"

"Make my own bed? *Myself?* For a whole *year*?" The princess looked quite faint.

"So, which is it?" snapped the king. "Did they kidnap you or not? Because if they did, we're taking them off right now for torture."

Everybody looked at the princess.

Nicola spun the handcuff—which was sized for a Globa-gaskarian adult, not an Earthling child—back and forth like a bracelet. Would the princess make such a big sacrifice for her new friends? It was a real test of friendship and Nicola suspected that the princess would fail it.

Finally the princess spoke up. "I'll tell you the truth."

37

THEY DIDN'T KIDNAP ME," SAID THE PRINCESS.
"As if they could kidnap me! Look at them! They're
so tiny, they barely reach my knees! Even Shimlara is short! I was bored and lonely and I felt like
going with them on a trip to Earth. Actually, I *ran*
straight into their helicopter."

Well, that part is true, thought Nicola, *even though we
were tickling her at the time.* In fact, it was easier than they'd
expected. Maybe it really *was* true?

There was silence.

"Uncuff the prisoners," ordered the king.

Nicola slid off her handcuff and handed it back to the
guard.

"You were *lonely*." The queen pressed a hand dramatically to her heart. "Our Nelly was *lonely*! Oh, dear, that's
a *tragedy*! Darling, you must come with us right now on the
rest of our vacations!"

"She can't have a vacation! She's being punished!"
boomed the king.

"Actually, I'd rather stay here on the beach for the
night," said the princess.

"We'll make sure *Nelly* makes her bed in the morning," said Sean. "We'll even give her some extra chores if you like. Make her work extra hard."

"Well, I guess you can stay here for one night, Nelly," said the queen, looking around the beach doubtfully. "Shall we arrange for a few dozen servants to stay with you?"

"That's okay," said Nicola firmly. "We don't need servants here."

"Fancy living without servants!" The queen ruffled Nicola's hair playfully.

"Speaking of which," Georgio rubbed his wrists where the handcuffs had been. "May I respectfully suggest you call off the garbage dumping, due to begin tomorrow morning? Otherwise, your daughter may wake up in a pile of garbage!"

"Yes, good thinking." The king flicked his hand at the chief guard. "You there, take care of that."

The guard rushed off.

"Work, work, work," said the king. "I never get a moment's rest. I think as soon as we get back home, it will be high time we treated ourselves to a nice, restful vacation, don't you agree, dear?"

"Oh yes," said the queen. "I'm *exhausted*. Shall we give you people a lift back to Globagaskar?"

"That would be very kind," said Mully.

"Unless, of course, you'd like us to stay with the Space Brigade here on the beach?" Georgio looked at Nicola brightly. "I wouldn't mind trying one of those mershmullows. Squid is staying with his grandma, so we've got the night free now we're not going to jail!"

Nicola thought for a second. There were times when you wanted adults around. There were other times when you just wanted to be alone.

Then she saw the hopeful look in Georgio's eyes and thought about all he and Mully had done to help save Earth. They'd spent hours collecting signatures for their petitions. They'd risked their lives for Earthlings! She knew there was only one answer.

"Of course you can," she said, and Georgio immediately launched into a celebratory chicken dance, while Shimlara covered her embarrassed face with both hands.

38

THE EARLY MORNING SUN WAS WARM ON NICOLA'S face. A gentle salty breeze lifted her hair from her forehead. Some nice person was already up and frying bacon. It smelled delicious.

She stretched out luxuriously in her sleeping bag without opening her eyes. There were two things to be happy about today. It was her birthday, and best of all the mission was complete.

Last night, after the king and queen had left in their giant spaceship, Greta had made another huge, crackling fire, which dried their clothes in a snap. Then they'd drunk mugs of creamy hot chocolate and eaten Tim Tams, while Georgio and Mully had told them about how they'd tricked the palace guards for hours by racing around Globagaskar with Molly Smith's redheaded daughter pretending to be the kidnapped princess in the back of the car.

"Hmm, I think we might need to employ some smarter guards," the princess had said.

They had also explained that it was Mully who had been responsible for tracking down the king and queen on the Planet of Doom.

"All the time the Committee was convincing people to sign petitions, Mully had a covert operation underway to find the king and queen," Georgio had boasted. "She had some of her old army buddies working undercover to make contact with them. We knew they'd put a stop to the princess's ridiculous plans for turning Earth into a garbage can—oh, excuse me, Princess Petronella."

"It's okay," the princess had said. "It was a pretty ridiculous idea."

After that, Georgio had tried to tell them ghost stories that weren't scary at all and Mully had told them a story about being in the army that actually *was* pretty scary. Then they had tucked themselves into their sleeping bags on the sand under the stars. The princess had snored like some sort of wild animal and Shimlara couldn't stop laughing, but Nicola had been so tired, she'd fallen into a deep, dreamless sleep right away.

Now it was morning. She was a year older. Everything was perfect.

"OH NO! HERE COMES THE GARBAGE!" shouted someone and at the same moment something cold and greasy landed *splat* on Nicola's face.

She opened her eyes in panic. Had the mission failed after all? She wriggled around desperately in her sleeping bag, trying to get to her feet.

"Happy birthday, Nic." Sean picked up the sandy piece of bacon he'd just thrown in her face.

"Thanks a lot," growled Nicola and wiped her cheek. "You nearly gave me a heart attack."

She realized her countdown watch was beeping and flashing like crazy. It said:

ALERT! ALERT!
NO TIME REMAINING! NO TIME REMAINING!
IS MISSION COMPLETE? IS MISSION COMPLETE?
ALERT! ALERT!
NO TIME REMAINING! NO TIME REMAINING!
IS MISSION COMPLETE? IS MISSION COMPLETE?
(BY THE WAY, HAPPY BIRTHDAY, EARTHLING AMBASSADOR!)
IS MISSION COMPLETE?
(BY THE WAY, HAPPY BIRTHDAY, EARTHLING AMBASSADOR!)

Nicola unstrapped the watch. From now on, it would be nice just to see the time when she looked at her wrist.

"Here's your special birthday breakfast." Katie handed Nicola a plate of fried eggs, bacon, mushrooms, and toast. "Hey, take a look over there." She pointed at a group of small children playing Frisbee near the water's edge—except it wasn't a Frisbee, it was the princess's silver tiara sparkling in the sun as they threw it back and forth.

"Where is the princess?" asked Nicola with her mouth full.

"She and Dad are boogie boarding," said Shimlara. "She didn't even bother to ask the kids for her tiara back."

Nicola looked out at the ocean and saw the princess and Georgio whooping as they both caught the same wave. The boogie board was too short for Georgio and his long legs flipped over his head as he went flying.

Mully shook her head. "My husband is quite insane."

Georgio's head popped up from under the water and he caught sight of Nicola. "It's the birthday girl!" he shouted and came running in from the water so fast his boogie board flew behind him like a kite. The princess followed.

"Is it time for presents?" she asked enthusiastically, dropping onto the sand on her wet knees.

"Oh, I don't think anybody has a present for me," said Nicola.

But she was wrong—*everyone* had a present for her.

The princess, who had heard from the others that it was Nicola's birthday, gave her a bracelet from her own wrist. It was a fine gold chain with red stones that glinted magically in the morning sun. It was too big for Nicola to wear as a bracelet, but it made a perfect necklace.

"Those are just a few very rare rubies," said the princess casually.

"Oh, lovely, thank you!" said Nicola, thinking, *FRIZZLE! I'd better not lose it!*

"It was Katie who reminded us that we'd probably be away for your birthday," said Tyler.

Katie, Tyler, and Sean had brought presents with them when Georgio had picked them up from Earth. Katie gave Nicola a gorgeous red top that went perfectly with her new ruby necklace, Tyler gave her a book by her favorite author, and Sean gave her the latest CD by *his* favorite band. "I'm just trying to improve your taste in music," he explained. "It's my duty as your brother."

Even Greta had gone down to the Buddy Beach pharmacy and bought Nicola a straw sun hat. "I thought you probably wouldn't want to get any more freckles," she said when Nicola opened it.

Georgio, Mully, and Shimlara were last.

It was something very large and flat, nearly as tall as Nicola, and wrapped up in brightly colored paper.

"We had bought it for you already on Globagaskar," said Mully. "I grabbed it when the guards came to capture us. I'm so glad we're not giving it to you in prison!"

Nicola gently tore off the paper. She had no idea what it could be.

It was a large round silver circle—like a gigantic coin—with two handles on either side.

"Oh, umm, thanks!" said Nicola confusedly.

"It's a *cloud-surfboard*!" explained Shimlara. "For when you go cloud-swimming. It's sort of like boogie boarding, but you skim across the clouds."

"Wow," said Sean jealously.

"And guess what? Later today we're having a Cloud Party for you, so you can try it out!" Georgio was so excited you would have thought it was his own birthday.

"But first," said Mully, "I expect your planet wants to say thank you." She pointed to a group of tiny dots in the sky and they heard the *chop-chop* sound of helicopters getting closer.

They all covered their heads as the helicopters landed in noisy mini-cyclones of sand. Nicola looked up and saw a group of people ducking under the helicopters' rotors and running across the sand.

It was her mom, her dad, and what looked like a whole pack of *prime ministers, presidents, kings, and queens* all heading toward *her*!

"Congratulations, Nicola and the whole Space Brigade," the prime minister of Australia bowed deeply. "You saved the world!"

"We are forever in your debt." The Queen of England actually curtsied!

Nicola looked around her and recognized famous faces

from television. All the leaders of the world were in one place! It seemed that the possibility of losing your planet really brought people together.

"If only you did your jobs around the house as well as you did this one, eh!" Nicola and Sean's dad ruffled their hair. Dads always made the most embarrassing jokes. They had a talent for it.

"Children, have you *cleaned your teeth*?" hissed Nicola's mom. "You're talking to royalty!"

Yep. Moms were just as embarrassing.

"I am curious, Nicola, what was the secret to your success?" asked a handsome young emperor. "Was it, perhaps, keen strategic thinking?"

Nicola thought for a moment.

Was there a secret? Was it just good luck?

Then it came to her.

"Friendship," she answered. "The secret was friendship."

"Ah." The emperor nodded and looked confused.

"It was friendship between planets. It was friendship between old friends and new friends." For a minute, Nicola felt herself swell with great wisdom. "It was friendship with older annoying brothers. It was even friendship with *enemies*!"

The world leaders all burst out into condescending laughter.

"Ha ha! Friendship! Good one!"

"If only it were that simple!"

"As if we could all just be friends like schoolchildren! Ha!"

Oh well.

"Now, we've organized a street parade to honor the Space Brigade and the Save the Little Earthlings Committee," explained the prime minister. "I believe that tall, lanky chap over there started the Committee?" He nodded at Georgio, who was currently walking on his hands along the beach much to the delight of a crowd of awed children.

"Yes, that's Georgio," said Nicola.

"I'd better go home before the parade." Princess Petronella came up quietly beside Nicola.

"And who is this young lady? Are you another of the kindly Globagaskarians who lobbied to save us from that evil princess?" asked the prime minister.

"Well, actually this *is* Princess Petronella," said Nicola. The world leaders gave a collective gasp.

"It's okay," said the princess. "Nicola and the Space Brigade convinced me not to turn your planet into a garbage can, although I might declare war on you if Sean doesn't stop teasing me."

A rather fragile prime minister put a hand to her forehead and fainted right into the Queen of England's arms, while a red-faced president puffed his chest out and said, "Bring it on, girlie!"

"For heaven's sakes, she's only *joking*!" said Nicola hastily. "And of course, you must join us for the parade, Princess Petronella! We insist!"

A short time later, Nicola, the princess, and the rest of the Space Brigade stood together on an open-topped car, driving through the streets of the city, listening to the grateful roar of the crowd, and waving to people as if they were celebrities—which they were, actually.

Georgio had organized for the Wardrobewhizonics to pay a quick visit and they'd organized cloud-swimming outfits for everyone to wear to Nicola's birthday party that afternoon. The girls' dresses shone richly in the sunlight, while the boys wore long black coats like Georgio had worn when he took Nicola cloud-swimming, along with wraparound dark glasses. Nicola couldn't wait to introduce them all to their first belly flop on a cloud.

In the back of the car, Georgio, Mully, and Nicola's mom and dad were getting along famously.

"You must come along to our place for a barbecue," said Nicola's mom.

"Delighted!" said Georgio. "What's a barbecue?"

Behind them was another car packed with all the other members of the Save the Little Earthlings Committee. Nicola could see Mr. Puck with the parrot on his shoulder squawking "Hooray! Hooray!" and freckly Molly Smith together with her redheaded daughter who had pretended to be the princess. There was Pamela George, the color expert who loved purple, wearing a celebratory new purple ball gown, and Ileria the astrologer giving the crowd a mystical wave. Rory Racrory, the letterologist who liked the letter *r*, was smiling broadly, while policeman Sergeant Tom Atkins looked grimly happy with his arms folded across his enormous chest. And of course, there was the very ordinary-looking psychic Ella Bell who had correctly predicted that something significant would happen on a beach beginning with the letter *B*.

As Nicola waved to the crowd, she realized it was only three days ago that she'd sat in Mrs. Zucchini's class trying to learn how to master mental telepathy in the hopes of making her birthday more memorable. It seemed like a million years ago. Since then, she'd traveled in space, kidnapped a princess, battled hungry alien creatures, and made new friends. She looked up at the sky. Instead of seeing garbage falling, she could see thousands of brightly colored streamers raining down and, above that, swirly gold and white clouds she'd be surfing on later. Nicola grinned. There was no doubt about it. This had turned out to be her most memorable birthday yet.

THE END

P.S. ONE MORE LITTLE THING YOU MIGHT LIKE TO KNOW . . .

UST AS THEY WERE COMING TO THE END OF THE parade, one of the streamers fell straight into Nicola's hand. To her surprise, there was a gold envelope attached to it with her name written in thick black letters: NICOLA BERRY.

Curious, she opened it. There was a white card inside. It said:

Dear Nicola,

    I understand you're the leader of a brigade of highly trained intergalactic freedom fighters and that you recently saved a planet by the name of EARTH.

    Our small but exquisite planet is currently facing grave danger of a rather unusual kind and we would like to engage your services. Payment would be both generous and delicious.

    If you are available and interested in taking on a new mission, please don't hesitate to call this number: 9028560824845093425089051808912309438O9421.

```
        We look forward with much anticipation
    to hearing from you,
                            COMMANDER IN CHIEF,
                            PLANET OF SHOBBLE
```

Nicola put the card back in the envelope and looked at the other members of the Space Brigade. Would they be interested in taking on another mission?

She had a feeling the answer would be a very definite ... YES.

LIANE MORIARTY

had her first story published when she was ten years old. Her mother still thinks it's the best thing she's ever written. Since then she's written seven novels for adults set in the real world and three books for children set in outer space. Some of her books have been number one best sellers and one has even been made into a TV series.

When she is not writing, she's either eating chocolate, reading in the bathtub, or standing on the side of the soccer field yelling out helpful advice to her children, even though she actually has no idea how to play.